CONSUMED

S. E. GREEN

Copyright © S. E. Green, 2025

The right of S. E. Green to be identified as the author of this work has been asserted per the Copyright, Designs and Patents Act 1976. All rights reserved. No part of this publication may be reproduced, transmitted, or stored in a retrieval system, in any form or by any means, without permission in writing from the publisher, nor be otherwise circulated in any form of binding or cover other than that in which it is published and without a similar condition being imposed on the subsequent purchaser. All characters in this publication are fictitious and any resemblance to real people, alive or dead, is purely coincidental.

1

A deep ravine slashed through a wooded area that stretched for miles through Claire Quade's East Tennessee neighborhood. Her running shoes pounded the dirt path and her bare thighs ached. Sweat trailed her neck as her ponytail bounced lightly. Her jaw clenched with determination at the last half mile.

Claire's pace quickened as she approached a narrow creek. Her stride didn't hesitate when she gracefully leaped over the water. She slowed then, coming to a clearing that led up a hill, into a backyard, and onto the deck of a white wood home. She checked her watch, smiling at the excellent results.

Breathing heavily, she stopped on the deck to stretch. Her gaze traveled up, seeing Kelsey, her daughter, through the kitchen window prepping morning coffee. Kelsey caught sight of her and smiled. Claire smiled back. With Kelsey's long brown hair, hazel eyes, and freckles, it was like looking into a mirror.

Inside, air conditioning soothed Claire's heated skin. She wedged her running shoes off and joined Kelsey in the kitchen where she poured herself a tall glass of filtered water and gulped the whole thing.

"Time?" Kelsey asked.

"Best yet," Claire said. "I'm definitely on track to run the marathon."

Still in pajamas, Kelsey slow-poured hot water over freshly ground beans. A pleasing aroma filled the air.

Claire chose a banana from the hanging fruit basket, peeled it, and took a bite. "Thought we might hit Target later today or tomorrow. You still need a few things for school. I can't believe you're going to be a high school senior."

"Dad texted me, asking if I wanted his old phone. Is it okay if I say yes?"

"Of course. You don't need to ask."

Brian, Kelsey's father, and Claire had been amicably divorced for five years now.

"Okay, good. Also, a little birdie told me someone's turning forty next week."

Claire laughed.

"What do you want to do?" Kelsey handed a steaming mug to Claire.

"A rom-com and junk food."

"You always want to do that!"

"Oh, and a giant piece of carrot cake."

"Believe me, I've already got that covered."

Claire pulled Kelsey in for a hug. "I love you."

"I love you, too, Mom."

Now dressed for work in a dark pencil skirt, modest heels, and a white button-down blouse, Claire beeped open her brand-new white Lexus. She'd worked hard to put the money aside and pay cash for her dream ride.

Once settled inside the rich brown leather interior, she eyed the garage door. This weekend, she promised herself, she would finally clear it out. The Lexus deserved indoor parking.

She backed out of her driveway, noting the brick house that shared her cul-de-sac had a moving truck parked outside, busy unloading furniture. It wasn't even on the market when it sold. According to her neighbors, some business man from out of town made an offer they couldn't pass up. Claire hoped the new owner jived with their quiet street.

She drove through her neighborhood of modest sized, older homes, all with neatly tended yards on spacious lots. She turned on the radio, choosing something soft, and navigated through her small town, eventually segueing onto the highway that would take her to work in Chattanooga.

As she drove, she rehearsed her presentation. Her midsize law firm had just merged with another smaller one, and the managing partner from both had asked her to handle the consolidation. If this went smoothly, Claire would be one step closer to being offered the open senior slot.

———

The presentation went better than expected. After, Claire mingled with the office staff and other lawyers. Fran, her executive assistant, approached carrying a small plate filled with sliced fruit, chopped vegetables, and cheese. Claire hoped that was for her. She was starving.

Five years older than Claire, Fran had been her executive assistant since Claire came on board—ten years ago now—as the firm's specialist in contract law. Fran was also Claire's great friend.

"You look hungry." Fran handed over the plate.

"You know me too well." Claire put her tea down and eagerly dug in. "Well?"

Fran grinned. "Seriously so good. A reorganization and merger presentation is no fun. You came across comfortable, well-spoken, and approachable. Everyone is calm now. We all thought layoffs were coming. Sure, we're being shifted around, but it's doable."

"Oh, good, I'm so glad. And PS, you're not being shifted around; you're staying with me."

"I expected nothing less." Fran snatched a strawberry from Claire's plate and munched. "Speaking of you, between this and that magazine article you were featured in I smell a promotion coming on."

Claire chuckled. "Don't jinx me." She scanned the room. "I'm not used to so many people. By the way, thank you for helping me choose who goes to the new floor. Everyone seems pleased."

"It had to be a mix of both firms and also personalities. And it helps that you and I are going to the new floor. People like it when the primary office sacrifices for those coming in. Thank you for being open to a smaller space."

"For sure." Claire ate a few pieces of cheese as she continued scanning the crowd. Giggles over to the right drew her attention where several of the younger hires gathered around, chatting. Claire continued eating, taking in the reception.

Her gaze passed right over him before pausing and circling back. There in the corner next to a fake tree stood a man dressed in a well tailored light gray suit with polished wing tip shoes. He wore his dark hair short and neatly styled and had a trim beard. From the fit of his shirt over a defined chest and biceps, he clearly worked out. She placed him about her age—late thirties/early forties. And though nearly thirty feet separated them, his eyes bore into hers.

Instinctively, her pulse kicked in and her face heated. Claire swallowed a surprisingly nervous lump. He lifted a coffee cup in a silent salute. Claire managed a small smile and a nod.

Oblivious to the exchange, Fran shifted, blocking Claire's view of the alluring man. "Did you pack your lunch?"

"I, um..." Claire blinked, refocusing on Fran. "I'm sorry, what?"

"Did you pack your lunch?"

"Oh, yeah, no. I'm taking you out to lunch to thank you for helping me with all of this."

Fran brightened. "You're on." She glanced around the room. "Guess I'm going to make the rounds, welcome the new firm. See you for lunch."

Fran wandered off, and Claire's gaze immediately darted back over to the corner. But the incredibly handsome man was gone.

Loaded down with red bullseye Target bags, Claire and Kelsey pulled into their driveway.

"Actually will you park on the street?" Kelsey said. "I want to shoot some hoops."

While running was Claire's thing, basketball was Kelsey's and she was good. So good in fact, she'd already been scouted by several colleges. They both expected scholarship offers soon.

Claire parked on the street, and as they began unloading, Kelsey added, "I saw the moving truck next door."

Claire glanced at the brick house. The place sat quiet with no lights on. "Yeah, me too."

Kelsey shut the trunk of the car. "Maybe in a few days we should go introduce ourselves."

"We can do that."

Later, after they had carted the Target haul in and ate grilled chicken for dinner, Kelsey flicked on the exterior lights and spent nearly an hour shooting hoops. The soft sound of the smack against the house once annoyed Claire but now filled her with melancholy. All too soon Kelsey would be off to college and Claire knew she'd miss that sound. The installation of the hoop over the garage had been done by Brian years ago when Kelsey was just a tiny girl. Brian had been shooting hoops one night when Kelsey wandered out. Soon, she was dribbling circles around him and making unbelievable shots. Neither realized what a gifted player she would become.

In the laundry room, Claire opened the dryer and pulled everything out, separating her things from Kelsey's. She delivered a warm pile to her daughter's room, noting her hamster, Louie, out of his cage, sitting on the windowsill and looking out at Kelsey playing basketball.

"You little Houdini. How do you do that?" Claire pet his little body, not bothering to put him back in. He'd just get out again. His whiskers twitched as he looked up at her through knowing eyes.

In her bedroom, Claire began putting her laundry away. As she placed her folded underwear into its drawer, her gaze lingered on a pile of sexy lingerie that Fran insisted she buy a year after the divorce.

"You need to get back out there," Fran had said. "Your vagina is going to dry up."

"Don't be so crass!" Claire had responded, laughing.

Fran also gifted Claire her very first vibrator.

That had been four years ago now and though the vibrator had seen plenty of action the lingerie had seen little to none. But Claire kept it anyway.

Her second-story bedroom's side window looked out over the side yard and house next door, now with lights on. She began to swivel her blinds closed for the night when the silhouette of an athletic man caught her eye as he moved from room to room carrying boxes. Through his own half closed blinds, she couldn't make out much more than he had dark hair. Idly, Claire scanned all the windows, not seeing anyone else.

Kelsey came in for the night, calling up the stairs, "Mom, you want ice cream?"

"Sounds good!" Claire swiveled the blinds closed and went down to the kitchen for Ben & Jerry's with her daughter.

Claire sat in her new smaller office, a glass of water on a nearby coaster, eyeballs deep in a contract when knuckles rapped softly on her door. She glanced up to see Fran grinning wickedly.

"Someone's here to see you," Fran said a little too eagerly.

"O...kay..."

Fran stepped aside. The dark haired man with the trim

beard appeared. Today he wore a white dress shirt with a green tie that perfectly matched his eyes. Those eyes smiled first, followed by only one corner of his mouth. It had to be the sexiest little grin Claire had ever seen. He stepped into her office, filling the space with his masculinity.

Claire cleared her throat and stood, smoothing her hands down her formfitting, sleeveless sweater dress.

The man extended his hand. "Wanted to introduce myself. I'm Dominic Voss."

Claire took his hand, finding it warm and strong. "Claire Quade. Nice to meet you."

He held the shake a fraction longer than normal. "I saw you yesterday but had to leave for a meeting, so I didn't get a chance to say hello."

Claire couldn't take her eyes off of him as she motioned him to sit. An invitation he declined. "I only have a second," he said. "Like I said, just wanted to say hi. I'm looking forward to working together."

Claire searched her brain for Dominic Voss in the merger documents, recalling his information. "You're the newest hire, specializing in family law. Moved here from Nashville."

"Correct. And you're our contract person, been here ten years."

"Yes."

His eyes smiled again. "Like I said, only a second. Nice to meet you, Claire Quade."

"Likewise."

He offered one last look that lingered much like his handshake before turning to leave. On her wall hung the framed magazine article she'd been featured in. He paused to look at it. "That's right. I knew you looked familiar. I read that. Nice piece."

"Thanks."

"Okay, see ya later." Then with a tiny wave, he disappeared from her office.

Fran instantly reappeared, closing the door behind her. "Um, okay. He's hot."

Still standing, Claire stared at the door.

And she stared.

And she continued to stare.

Fran said something else, but her words didn't register in Claire's brain. Slowly, she sat, picking up her long forgotten glass of water and drinking nearly half of it. She placed it back on its coaster, swiveling away to look out the window behind her and the blue expanse of sky. Fran stepped into her line of vision and Claire shifted her gaze over to her friend's amused, and knowing, expression.

"What?" Claire said.

Fran suppressed a grin. "Well, Claire Quade, I do declare, you officially have an office crush."

With a groan, Claire covered her heated face with her hands. "This is so not good."

Fran let out a cute, but evil giggle. "Says who? You're hot, he's hot. He's not wearing a wedding band. And don't give me that, 'I don't date people I work with' thing. Hell, I'll do him."

Claire gave her a withering look. "You're married."

Fran shrugged. "A technicality."

Claire laughed. "All right, scat. I need to get back to work."

With a salute, Fran headed out. And Claire sat entirely too long thinking about Dominic Voss.

2

That night, Claire stood waist deep in the boxes and various junk filling her garage. The automatic door was open, letting in cool night air as Kelsey performed layups just outside.

With a box cutter, Claire opened a carton labeled "Childhood Things." Right on top rested the Cabbage Patch knockoff her mom had made her with Claire's name stitched into the doll's blue dress. Claire picked it up, running her fingers over the material, smiling at the childhood memory of when she opened the Christmas present. She'd screamed and danced with excitement, and her mom just giggled and giggled.

With her phone, Claire snapped a picture and texted it to her mom who immediately texted back with a heart emoji.

Claire never knew her dad but she got along famously with her mom who had recently moved to a retirement community not far from Chattanooga. Claire tried to visit her a few times per month if she could.

She put her phone down and looked at the various piles

she'd sorted over the past hour going to Goodwill, Habitat for Humanity, and also the keep pile. Unfortunately, the keep pile was bigger than the other two combined. Not that Claire considered herself a hoarder, but she did find it hard to part with things.

Which was why Kelsey was so valuable. Claire's daughter had a practical side Claire lacked.

She held the doll up for Kelsey to see. "Verdict?"

"Keep," Kelsey said, running a layup.

Claire gladly placed it on top of the other things in that pile.

"Claire?" a man's voice stated.

She glanced past Kelsey and into the night where Dominic Voss stood in the cul-de-sac. Dressed in a sleeveless tee and athletic shorts, he held the leash of a friendly looking chocolate lab.

She didn't immediately respond. Why was he here in her neighborhood?

Kelsey stopped playing basketball. She looked from Claire to Dominic and back to Claire. "Mom?"

Claire came to, stepping from the garage into the night. The confusion must have been all over her face because Dominic said, "I didn't realize you lived here." He nodded to the brick house next door. "I just moved in."

Kelsey waved. "Hi, I'm Kelsey."

A nervous chuckle fluttered through Claire's chest. "Sorry. This is my daughter. Kelsey, this is Dominic Voss. Aside from our neighbor, he's new to my office."

Kelsey smiled. "Cool. Can I say hi to your dog?"

"Of course." Dominic came up the driveway. "This is Oscar."

As Dominic watched Kelsey greet Oscar, Claire allowed her gaze to travel down Dominic's muscular body, tracing the curve of his shoulders and biceps, the stretch of the tee over his chest, and his defined thighs as he, too, crouched down to rub Oscar's head.

Her appreciative gaze finished its perusal, and her eyes lifted to find Dominic doing the same to her. She did a mental check of her own casual attire, glad she'd put on a pair of running shorts and a tank. She didn't consider herself vain but Claire knew she had a decent, athletic body and wasn't afraid to show it now and then.

Claire closed the distance between them, leaning down to greet Oscar. "Aren't you sweet?"

"You've got quite the project in that garage," Dominic said.

She came upright, maintaining eye contact with him. His green eyes smiled, followed by the one corner of his mouth. Surreptitiously, she inhaled his scent—a mixture of soap, laundry detergent, and something uniquely him. Claire could not recall ever having such an intoxicating reaction to a man before.

"It's been on Mom's to-do list forever," Kelsey said.

Dominic eyed the garage. "Looks like you have some heavy stuff in there. If you need help, just ask."

"I will," Claire said. "Thank you."

Dominic backed away. "Well, I'll leave you two to your evening."

"Hey, Mr. Voss," Kelsey called out, "if you ever need a dog walker, I'm available. I walk a lot of dogs in the area. I even have references."

"It's Dominic and I'll take you up on that." His amused eyes met Claire's. "I'll likely be working long hours. I hear the people at my new firm are real workhorses."

Claire laughed. "Not true. We're all about work-life balance."

"Good to know." With Oscar in tow, Dominic walked off.

Kelsey went back to playing basketball and Claire watched Dominic walk the short distance to his new home. He climbed the few steps up to his porch and as he opened the front door, he glanced back, and Claire quickly looked away.

Why she looked away, she didn't know. She should have just owned it and waved.

Later in her bedroom, she went about her nightly routine—washing her face, brushing and flossing, putting on pajamas, and picking out tomorrow's outfit. When she approached her side window to close the blinds, she lingered, watching Dominic walk through his house, his own half-closed blinds offering a tantalizing peek of his movements.

Claire swiveled hers shut, took her vibrator from its drawer, and closed her eyes as she pleasured herself to thoughts of Dominic Voss—the enticing new neighbor and co-worker.

———

Early the next morning, Claire's feet ate up the trail that ran behind the neighborhood. Through the overcast sky, the sun just barely offered morning light. A slight rain began to patter, dampening her clothes and cooling off her heated muscles.

Her watch beeped, indicating she needed to pick up her pace for one final push. She did, rounding the last bend and leaping a downed tree. Her chest rose and fell with heavy breaths and her heart thud heavy.

Her watch once again beeped—signaling she needed to

begin slowing her stride. She did, pressing her fingers to her throat, counting the beats. She glanced at her watch, smiling, pleased with her time. Gradually, she moved into a walk.

"You training for something?"

Claire came to an abrupt stop. On the trail just paces away stood her new neighbor, dressed for work, holding an umbrella and doggie bags, watching Oscar explore the area.

She wiped sweat and rain from her chin. "I'm running a marathon next weekend."

"Wow, impressive."

"Thanks."

Claire looked at his work clothes. "You're going in early."

"I am, yes." Dominic glanced at her legs. "I figured you were a runner. Have you always been?"

"Pretty much. I'm sure one day my knees will hate me but for now I keep at it."

"Perhaps some morning I'll join you."

Claire liked that idea a lot, but still, she found herself saying, "I'd say sure but I'm in training mode so my runs are a bit focused."

"Got it. Maybe after the marathon."

She should have continued walking and cooling off, but she didn't. Something shifted in the air between them, going from the friendliness of a second ago to a buzzing awareness. Dominic's eyes traveled down her wet clothes clinging to her body. She didn't shrink from his gaze as he moved a fraction, putting her under the umbrella. They hovered dangerously close to one another, looking into each other's eyes.

Her watch beeped and Claire pulled back. "That's, um, that's my cue that I need to get ready for the day."

She offered a smile and a wave, lightly jogging the rest of the way to her house. As she trotted up onto the back deck, she glanced toward the trail, hoping to catch him looking—as he had caught her last night—but he'd already wandered off, following Oscar.

Inside, Kelsey sat at the kitchen island, texting and drinking coffee. She'd already poured Claire a tall glass of tepid water that she eagerly drank.

"Can I spend the weekend with June?" Kelsey put her phone down. "Her parents are taking her older sister back to college and she doesn't want to be alone all weekend."

Two teenage girls alone in a house for a weekend. Many parents wouldn't allow it but Claire one hundred percent trusted Kelsey. She'd never done anything to lose that trust. "Fine by me," Claire said. "Promise me you'll eat a lot of junk food and talk about boys."

Kelsey laughed. "Deal." Another text came in that she quickly read. "June also wants to know if we can make a batch of your 'garbage' cookies for me to take over."

Garbage cookies as in oatmeal-dark chocolate-peanut butter-macadamia nut-cranberry-white chocolate-Nutella. The cookies came about quite by accident. Kelsey had been ten at the time and hosting a slumber party. The girls started dumping everything in the pantry into the mix, surprising Claire with how good they actually turned out. So good, in fact, seven years later and her friends still talked about—and requested—them.

"That we can do." Claire finished her water, grabbed her daily banana, and headed upstairs.

In the shower, she soaped her body. She thought about all the things to be done today at work. She was just about to rinse when her thoughts shifted...to Dominic. As they did, her movements slowed. Her hands slid over her skin, gliding through the suds, pressing in, massaging. Her fingers found their way between her legs, and this time no vibrator was needed.

When she'd dried off and began dressing her phone buzzed with a text.

> Fran: Don't forget we're double-dating tonight. And don't even think about canceling. We already have a reservation for 6. We'll leave from work. PS: I already texted Kelsey because I knew you'd forget.

Claire reread the text, briefly wondering if she could ask Kelsey to play sick so that she could stay home and "care" for her. But she knew that wouldn't fly. She texted Fran a thumbs up and hoped to God this blind date was better than the last Fran set her up with.

Claire caught herself looking for Dominic Voss throughout the day. Not that she walked the hallways, actively searching him out. But when she went to the restroom, she passed by his office, glancing in, and disappointedly finding it empty. During a coffee break, she did the same thing, and while she took the stairs down one floor to a meeting, she found herself searching for a glimpse.

She felt like she was in high school again, enamored with a boy. She should feel silly, but she didn't. She enjoyed the apparent infatuation she carried for this man.

Eventually, Claire's brain refocused, the day rolled on, and the time came to leave for the double date.

Now here she sat with Fran and her husband, Sean, in an upscale Italian restaurant. They laughed at something

Claire's date, Matt, just said. Claire smiled to be polite but my God was she bored.

Matt was, she supposed, a catch. Just not her catch. He worked as a superintendent for a construction company and knew Sean from a local baseball league. In his early forties with salt-and-pepper hair, Matt had a nice smile and a decent sense of humor. Divorced with a ten-year-old son he clearly adored, Matt checked a lot of boxes: educated, employed, well-groomed, good conversationalist...

Maybe another time, another place, Claire would've been into Matt, but her brain kept drifting to the garage cleanup she needed to finish; emails to be returned; client meetings to prep for; and a myriad of other things.

When you're on a date and thinking about work, something's off. It wasn't that Claire considered herself a workaholic—she believed in balance—but tonight she'd rather that balance be back home doing pretty much anything but this.

Oh, yeah, she also needed to bake those garbage cookies for Kelsey.

Eventually, the check came. Matt picked up the entire tab—which he absolutely did not have to do—and walked Claire out.

Gentleman. Another box he checked.

"Well, Claire, it's been a delight." Matt shook her hand. "Thank you for a lovely evening."

Polite. Yet another box.

"And thank you. You did not have to pay for the bill. That was very kind of you." Claire smiled, suddenly feeling bad for not being completely present. Matt really was a nice man. "I'm sorry if I came across as distracted. I've got a lot on my mind."

With a good-natured smile, he took her hand again, kissing the backside of it. "Perhaps we'll try again, just the two of us."

"You know what, I'd like that," she said and meant it.

With a friendly nod, he walked across the parking lot toward his car.

Fran stepped up, her arm linked through Sean's. "What is wrong with you? He's great. You were everywhere but here tonight. Claire, I love you, but you are like the worst date ever. You barely even spoke."

"I know." Claire sighed. "I'm sorry. Maybe no more double dates for a bit. Okay?"

"Okay." Fran hugged her and walked off with Sean.

Claire slid into the slick and luxurious interior of her Lexus and drove the thirty minutes or so home, taking her time, enjoying back roads and some Fleetwood Mac filtering through her speakers.

She pulled into her neighborhood and onto her street. As she neared her house, her eyes trailed to Dominic's place, finding his lights on. She also saw Brian's black Cherokee parked in her driveway. She didn't realize he was coming over tonight.

Light spilled from the open garage where he and Kelsey sifted through boxes. Kelsey caught sight of Claire, smiling and waving, and Brian did as well.

Brian and Claire met in college and became best friends. A year into that close friendship they began fooling around. At twenty-two, Claire turned up pregnant and Brian proposed. Much to both of their parents' dismay, they eloped in a cheesy Vegas thing. Nine months later, Kelsey came along. Claire went to law school and Brian graduated with a degree in history, going on to become a high school teacher.

Months turned to years, holidays and birthdays passed, they lived their lives, and then one day they realized quite amicably that while they did love each other, they had never been *in love* with each other. Their relationship was and would always be best friends. So, Brian moved out, the divorce came, they shared custody of Kelsey, and here they were five years later.

"Hey," Claire said, stepping into the garage. Her gaze touched on the piles of sorted items, noting a new section where Brian was currently placing a slow cooker.

With thick dark hair that never quite lay right, tortoise shell glasses, and a tall, lean body, Brian still looked like he did in college. "Hey, back," he said, adjusting his glasses. "I didn't think you'd mind. Kelsey said you were clearing things out."

"I don't mind at all. Take whatever you want."

"Mr. Voss!" Kelsey called out and waved. She trotted from the garage out into the night where Dominic stood with Oscar. Kelsey came down in front of him, rubbing his head.

Claire's pulse kicked in as she followed at a slower pace, fully aware of Dominic's green gaze rolling slowly over her. It was a perusal Claire felt in the marrow of her bones.

"Hello, Claire," he said.

"Dominic."

"You just getting home?" he asked.

"Mom had *a date*," Kelsey teased.

Heat rushed to Claire's face but her eyes stayed fixed on Dominic's as they smiled in that sexy way.

"Is that so?" he teased right back.

"Just a friend of a friend," Claire told him.

Kelsey kept loving on Oscar as Dominic and Claire stood, an almost electric tension between them. This was not in her head—this heat, this animal attraction—it had to be reciprocal.

"Hi." Brian stepped up beside Claire, extending his hand. "I'm Brian, Kelsey's father. You must be the new neighbor. Kelsey told me someone moved in."

Claire watched her ex and Dominic exchange pleasantries. My God, were they so very different—Brian with his bookish and very boy-next-door looks and Dominic with his confident and raw manliness that filled the space.

Dominic glanced toward the garage. "Well, looks like you all still have lots of work there." He backed away. "Have a good evening."

Claire wanted to watch him walk away, but she made herself turn and go back to the garage with her ex and her daughter.

Later, after Brian had left, Claire walked around her bedroom, her eyes flitting toward the blinds that faced Dominic's bedroom, hoping for a peek of him.

She was not disappointed.

His en suite bathroom door opened. With only a towel wrapped around his waist, he stepped into his bedroom. Claire quickly turned the lights off in her room and plastered herself to the wall beside her window. She was just about to look out the blinds when she realized the mirror affixed to the dresser on the opposite wall offered a view straight into Dominic's room.

She knew, absolutely knew, she was being a creepy voyeur but she couldn't stop herself. Hell, she didn't want to stop herself as she watched him walk around his space with just that towel and one hell of a sculpted chest. He moved to the blinds, his hand coming up to close them when he stopped.

And he stared.

Claire stopped breathing. She didn't even blink.

Dominic undid the towel and it slid to the floor. He stood for several seconds, silhouetted by the light, his lower body cast in a shadow. Then with that sexy smile that touched his eyes first before the corner of his lips, he rotated the blinds closed.

Claire remained frozen against the wall, staring at the mirror and the view of his closed blinds. There was no way he saw her, was there? No, he couldn't have known she was watching. Her lights were out. Not even a nightlight illuminated her room.

Which meant what? That he was hoping she was watching? He was fantasizing it? Inviting it?

Claire slid to the floor.

Holy hell. She'd never been so turned on in her life and they hadn't even touched.

She didn't know what kind of game he wanted to play —if any—but she hoped he did. And she knew without a doubt that she would play it with him.

3

The next day she saw Dominic everywhere. They were both in an hour-long morning meeting that bled over into lunch. In the afternoon, another meeting, followed by a required office training. They saw each other in the hallway, in the breakroom, in the elevator…

Throughout it all, they maintained a level of professionalism, only glancing each other's way or talking to the other when appropriate. But when they did, sexual energy filled the space between them to the point Claire wondered if others could feel it too.

She also could not stop imagining him naked.

At home that evening, she made Kelsey's garbage cookies and while they baked, she started dinner. Outside, Kelsey's basketball thumped softly against the driveway.

Claire moved around the kitchen, making spaghetti and meat sauce. She started to steam some broccoli when she realized Kelsey's playing had picked up pace. That, and the sound of muffled voices followed.

Had Brian returned? Claire wasn't anticipating him coming over that night.

She double-checked the stove before walking through the house and out the front door to discover Kelsey and Dominic in an all-out, one-on-one match with Oscar lying in the grass watching.

Dominic stole the ball, sidestepped Kelsey, spun the other way, and went to shoot when Kelsey blocked him. She took possession of the ball, dribbled further down the driveway, and did an overhand that didn't even hit the net as it went through.

"Dang, girl, you are good!" Dominic laughed.

It was the first time Claire had heard his laugh. Like everything else about him, it was sexy as hell. As was the curve of his butt in those athletic pants.

Kelsey caught sight of her. "Hey, Mom."

Dominic turned then, his eyes meeting hers, and breathing heavily, he smiled. Claire smiled back.

"Dinner ready?" Kelsey asked.

"Just about," Claire said.

Kelsey retrieved the ball, looking at Dominic. "Have you eaten?"

"No."

"Wanna stay?"

"If it's okay with your mom."

Claire did a fine job of hiding her grin. "It's more than okay."

Minutes later, the three of them sat at the kitchen table. Dominic helped himself to spaghetti, followed by one stalk of broccoli.

"Not a fan of green things?" Kelsey asked, helping herself to a generous portion of the vegetable. Even as a little girl, she loved all fruit and vegetables. It made feeding her easy.

"Unfortunately, broccoli is my least favorite thing on the planet Earth. Well, that's not true. Asparagus is my least favorite."

"Because it makes your pee stink?" Kelsey joked.

"Kelsey," Claire half-heartedly admonished.

Dominic laughed. "No, I just don't like the taste." He smiled at Claire across the table. "No offense to your broccoli."

"None taken," Claire said as she served herself. "So, what vegetables *do* you like?"

"Why, am I getting another dinner invitation?" Dominic teased.

"Maybe," Claire teased right back.

"I'm a big fan of spinach," he said. "Ever had it sautéed with pine nuts and tomatoes?"

Kelsey brightened. "Ooh, that does sound good."

Under the table, Oscar laid across Dominic's feet. As they continued to eat, Claire happily listened to Kelsey and Dominic talk. He had a great sense of humor, a sharp intellect about him, and when he laughed it crinkled the corners of his green eyes.

Kelsey reached under the table to rub Oscar's head. "He is really well behaved. We had a dog when I was younger and he was a mess. He destroyed Mom's shoes, he pooped everywhere but outside, and he barked nonstop. He drove us nuts, didn't he, Mom?"

"That he did," Claire agreed.

Dominic reached under the table to rub Oscar's head as well. "For one, he's old. But he's always been a good boy. No shoe destruction or unnecessary barking, and the only time he pooped indoors was a reactionary poop."

Kelsey smiled. "What's a reactionary poop?"

"The smoke alarm went off at one in the morning. It was so loud *I* nearly pooped."

The three of them laughed. Dominic's gaze trailed over to the island where the cookies sat cooling. "My curiosity has gotten the best of me. Those are the oddest cookies I have ever seen."

Claire surveyed them from a new eye and yes, the lumpy dark brown mounds did look odd. "They're 'garbage' cookies. We made them up years ago. They look gross, and they have about a million calories each, but they are beyond fantastic." Claire got up from the table and folded one in a napkin that she placed beside Dominic's plate. "For later."

"Or now." He took a bite, his amazed eyes meeting Kelsey's.

"I know, right?" she said.

"Oh my God." He ate another bite. And another.

Kelsey joined him, getting her own cookie, and Claire did as well. Dessert during dinner. Why not?

Conversation after that flowed from basketball to Kelsey's senior year of high school, from college plans to TV shows and books. Before any of them had realized it, time had ticked on and Kelsey began to hide her yawns.

Dominic took his plate to the sink. "Can I help clean up?"

"There's really nothing to do other than load the dishwasher," Claire said. "But thank you."

Dominic took his phone out. "Mind if we exchange numbers?"

Claire rattled off hers and he plugged it into his phone. "Well, goodnight. Thank you again for dinner and the company. I hope we can do it again."

"For sure."

"What is this?" Kelsey asked, holding up Dominic's keychain that he had left on his placemat.

"Press it and see," he said.

She pressed a tiny black button on a flat, vibrant-red rectangular object. One end lit up brighter than any flashlight Claire had ever seen.

"Cool! I could totally use this." Kelsey showed Claire. "Will you get me one?"

"I'll buy both of us one. That *is* cool."

Dominic crossed the kitchen and took the flashlight from Kelsey. "Tell you what, I'll order you both one. Colors?"

"Green," Kelsey said at the same time Claire responded, "Purple."

"Got it." He pocketed it as he patted his leg for Oscar to get up.

Claire began loading the dishwasher as Kelsey walked Dominic to the front door.

Seconds later, Kelsey bounded back into the kitchen. "Mom, he is amazing. You two should totally go out."

Claire smiled, waving her off. "You need to get in bed. You've got an early practice in the morning."

"Yeah, yeah, yeah." Kelsey gave her a goodnight hug and headed to her room.

Minutes later, Claire entered her own room. She went straight to the blinds, ready to close them, promising herself she would not be a creepy voyeur when she once again caught sight of Dominic undressing.

This time she did not turn out her light or hide against the wall. No, she gave a little show of her own.

She still wore her clothes from work—dress pants and a sleeveless blouse—and took her time shedding both. Now down to just her bra and bikini style panties—a beige set trimmed in lace—she boldly walked around her room, pretending to do things that didn't need to be done—organizing a drawer, rearranging the books on her nightstand, looking through her jewelry box... All the while resisting the urge to glance at the window.

Eventually, she did, surreptitiously looking in the mirror that gave her a view of Dominic's room. And, sure enough, he stood there watching her.

With a tiny and very pleased smile, she walked into her en suite bathroom and closed the door.

On Friday, Claire spent the bulk of her day off-site visiting clients. She didn't see or even have much chance to think of Dominic.

A text came in from Kelsey.

> Kelsey: June's here. I'm headed out for the weekend, garbage cookies in tow.

> Claire: See you on Sunday. You start senior year bright and early Monday morning. Crazy!

> Kelsey: It is crazy. I love you. Bye-bye.

Claire sent her a smiley face emoji. Another text came in, this one from Fran.

> Fran: You coming back to the office or can I close things down?

> Claire: Nope, close away.

> Fran: In the mood for a Friday cocktail?

> Claire: Sure, but only one.

> Fran: Blah, blah, blah…

Claire laughed. Fran had a way of talking her into not only one strong martini but often more than one.

> Claire: Usual place?

Fran sent her a thumbs up emoji.

Claire arrived before Fran at the Mediterranean restaurant that made the best, and strongest, vodka martinis. She chose a high-top table for two and ordered two dry martinis with three olives each, followed by the pita appetizer that came with hummus, tahini, and spicy feta cheese dip.

Fran arrived not much later. She picked up her martini and delivered her usual raunchy toast. "Cheers to men who are big and those who are small. Cheers to men who think they're big but really aren't at all. And cheers to those who in the middle of the night go from small to big and stick it in us right."

They clinked glasses and sipped, both immediately digging into the appetizer.

After Claire got a bite or two down her, she boldly said, "Speaking of sticking it in us right…"

Fran was in the middle of a sip and nearly spit her

vodka. She scrambled to wipe her mouth, staring wide eyed, and quite frozen, at Claire.

Amused, Claire took another sip. "I've got this new neighbor. He moved in beside me."

Fran hurriedly waved her on.

"He's only been there a week and we've already had several encounters, as in friendly exchanges on the trail behind my house, in my driveway, and he came over last night for dinner."

"*Aaand?*"

"And things are super sexually charged between us. Like, we can't take our eyes off each other. There's this magnetic pull. Fran, I've never experienced anything like it." Claire paused, mostly because she knew it would drive Fran nuts. "Then there's the voyeurism he and I have going on."

Fran held her hand up. "Wait." She took a deep sip. Claire did the same.

Fran put her glass down. "Okay, continue."

Claire leaned in, lowering her voice. "Our bedroom windows are in line with each other. Two nights ago I turned my lights out and I watched him get naked. He was about to close his blinds and then just boldly stood there, staring out his window at mine. Last night I decided to give him a peek and did a bit of a striptease, walking around my room in my underwear."

"Please tell me you had on good underwear."

Claire smiled. "Oh yeah." She leaned in further, lowering her voice even more. "I've masturbated twice this week fantasizing about him."

Fran sat back fanning herself with both hands. Amused, Claire took another sip of her martini. Fran followed.

"Holy shit," Fran said. "This is so unlike you."

"I know. I don't know what has come over me but I'm going with it. Whatever little naughty adventure he wants, I'll reciprocate. Maybe I'll finally put that lingerie you made me buy to good use. Hopefully."

"Okay, so many questions. First, what is his name?"

Claire did not want Fran to know her new sexy neighbor was indeed their new coworker, so she lied. "Oakland."

"That's an unusual but kinda hot name." Fran ate an olive out of her martini. "Next question. What does he look like?"

"Well, he's about my age and around six feet tall. He has dark hair and such a fabulous body. Like the kind of body you get from taking care of yourself—eating right and exercising. Not like weightlifter big, but sculpted and muscular like...like..." Claire laughed at the comparison she was about to make. "Like he chops wood or something."

"A lumberjack. I can work with that. He'll be able to pick you up and throw you around."

They shared a giggle.

"He also has a fabulous sense of humor and the absolute sexiest, most manliest smile I have ever seen," Claire said. "And he smells..." Claire inhaled. "Like clean laundry, man, and the woods."

Fran sighed, longingly. "Oh, I bet he knows his way around a woman's body."

"I bet so too."

"Third question. What does he do for a living?"

"Government stuff," Claire lied.

"A spy. Cool."

Claire laughed. "No, not a spy."

"Kelsey's gone for the weekend. When was the last time you had sex?"

"That conference I went to six months ago." Claire made a face. "Not a very memorably encounter."

"You're past due then. Please tell me you are going to do the nasty."

Claire didn't hide her grin. "Oh, I hope so."

Fran fanned herself again. "I am vicariously living through you. Please, please, please don't make me wait until Monday. Text or call. I need deets."

Claire clinked her glass to Fran's. "If there are deets to share, you're my person."

"If you do another peep show, it's only fair to give him the whole view. After all, you did see *him* naked."

Heat rushed to Claire's face.

"Are you blushing? Don't get shy on me now. You have a fabulous body. Show it to him."

It wasn't shyness that flushed Claire, it was the daring thought of doing just that.

Later, when Claire arrived home, she noted all the lights out in Dominic's house. Being close to midnight, he'd likely gone to bed or perhaps he was out for the evening. Save from walking over and looking in his garage, there was no way to tell.

And perhaps that's what emboldened her as she turned on her bedside light, casting the room in a gentle glow. She left the blinds open. Across the way, Dominic's dark and lifeless window stared back.

She reached for the sash on her wraparound skirt, taking her time unknotting it and letting it slide to the floor. With it she wore a V-neck silk blouse that she slowly gathered and pulled over her head, allowing it to catch and swish her long brown hair.

She stood, unflinching, in a matching green set. Slowly, her hands traveled to the front of her bra. Her fingers didn't tremble as she unhooked the clasp and pulled it open. Her breasts met the air conditioning and tightened. Claire breathed heavily, electrified, and then she slid from her panties and stood naked, fully aroused.

For what seemed like an eternity, she stared out at Dominic's window, not feeling vulnerable at all. No, she felt empowered baring her body.

But...nothing happened. He could be in bed, or standing and watching. She didn't know, and half of her hoped he didn't see this little show while the other half hoped he did.

Finally, she swiveled the blinds shut and her body began to shake from the adrenaline. A nervous laugh shook through her. She gathered her clothes and sank onto the edge of her bed.

She'd never felt so alive, so sexy.

4

Saturday morning dawned and Claire promised herself she would finish the garage today. She made herself a cup of coffee and dug in.

An hour later, she'd sifted through the very last box, taping it shut, and labeling it "Goodwill." Loaded with cookware, Claire struggled to carry it from the garage to her Lexus. Bright sunshine beat down on her as she grunted, almost tripping over her feet. She was just about to heave the heavy box into her trunk when a shadow fell over her.

Dominic reached around her, easily taking the box from her hands and placing it next to a few others already in place and ready to go.

"Thank you," Claire said. "You're a lifesaver."

Dominic picked up a bag of bagels that he'd placed on the ground along with Oscar's leash. "We were out exploring the neighborhood." He held up the bag. "These any good?"

"Oh yeah. You made a good choice. Right beside that shop is a place that makes killer cold-pressed juices, if you're into that."

Dominic made a face.

Claire laughed. "Guess not." She studied his face for a hint that he saw her last night in the window but nothing seemed there.

"Why don't I help you finish loading and we'll share bagels?" he offered.

"Deal."

Over the next fifteen minutes, they loaded Claire's car down with everything going to Goodwill. Habitat for Humanity would come next week and pick up the remaining things. After that, Claire would officially have an indoor spot to park her pretty new car.

She closed the garage door and led him inside to the kitchen. "Thank you so much for the help."

"Not a problem. You hungry?"

"Starving."

Claire took out plates and utensils as Dominic unloaded a variety of bagels and cream cheese. She poured them both coffee and they sat side by side at the kitchen island, eating, stealing looks, smiling. Neither spoke. The silence should be uncomfortable but it wasn't.

Dominic finished his last bite of sesame bagel with cream cheese, following that with a sip of coffee. Then he looked up to the ceiling and the second floor beyond. "Kelsey still sleeping?"

"She's gone for the weekend."

Dominic brought his focus back to Claire. She held his gaze, licking cream cheese from her fingertip. He reached around her, releasing the band from her ponytail, letting her long hair graze his fingers. She imagined him tugging at it as he did. She grew aware of his breathing, each intake as they sat there, so close, really taking the other in.

He delicately touched his index finger to a faint round scar on Claire's temple. "Chicken pox?"

Claire swallowed. "Yes."

He caressed the scar, trailing his finger across one eyebrow, down the bridge of her nose, and softly across her bottom lip.

Claire didn't breathe.

He leaned in and his lips brushed her ear as he whispered, "You are sexy as fuck."

Claire did breathe then, one raspy intake, and with it the words, "We, um, work together."

"Is that going to be a problem?" he murmured, his breath hot.

Yes. No. Yes. "No, not if we don't make it."

"Then let's not make it." He kissed the spot just beneath her ear.

Claire shivered. "Okay."

She closed her eyes as his lips traveled further down, moving her T-shirt's collar aside and kissing her collarbone.

"What are you thinking, Claire?"

Her chest rose and fell. "My mind's a little blank right now."

His lips traveled up her neck, slowly kissing a path, finding their way to the corner of her mouth. "I saw you last night in the window."

Claire took his face in her hands and kissed him hungrily.

Dominic stood, roughly pulling her to her feet and pushing her up onto the kitchen island. Her legs parted and he pressed his body to hers. They groped each other, tearing at one another's clothes. Claire tugged the shirt he wore over his head. Dominic yanked her shorts down her legs.

Claire feverishly unbuttoned his jeans and wrenched his zipper down. She freed him right as he tore her panties.

Claire was just about to ask, "Condom?" when he entered her.

She didn't care. She fell back onto the island, scattering a bowl of apples. He pounded her hard and Claire moaned loudly. Her hands clutched at him, pulling him in, urging him to go harder still.

He did not disappoint.

She came fast. He did too.

Then...silence.

For a long moment, Dominic stayed inside of her, both struggling for breath, his face hidden in her breasts.

Eventually, he lifted his head and she opened her eyes. They stared at one another as he pulled out of her. He gripped her shirt, tugging her up to a sitting position, keeping his eyes fixed on hers the entire time.

Softly, he kissed her.

Next, he finished undressing her, sliding off her tee and undoing her bra. He stepped the rest of the way from his jeans and Claire slid from the island to the floor. Her fingers twined with his and she led him up the stairs and into her room.

Claire turned to face him but before she had a chance to register anything, he pushed her back onto the bed and came down on top of her. His lips, his hands, his tongue were all over her, touching her in ways she hadn't been touched in years. Maybe not ever.

Raw. Carnal. Uninhibited. Claire gave into it all as Dominic pleasured her to another climax.

When she had gained her breath, she rolled him to his back and crawled on top. She straddled him, grasping him and sinking down hard, riding him fast and urgently.

Dominic groaned as Claire arched her back, fondling her breasts, coming again. He flipped her over, kissing a path down her body, his mouth once again finding her core.

She didn't think she had a fourth orgasm in her but my God his tongue worked her, his fingers sliding inside and hooking up. Her fingers dug into his hair, her body coming off the mattress, and as she rode another release, he entered her again and found his own.

Later, and both satiated, they lay limply intertwined.

"So much for condoms," Dominic mumbled. "Sorry."

"My fault too."

"We'll be safer from here on out."

Claire loved that there would be a "here on out."

Dominic ran a lazy finger down her body. "Oh, the things I have in mind."

With her eyes still closed, Claire smiled. "Do tell."

"Nope. Many surprises to come." He crawled off of her, pulling her with him as he did. "Shower."

He led her into the bathroom and she turned on the shower. He pulled her to the mirror, standing behind her as she stared at her tangled hair and the flushed skin where his beard brushed.

Dominic started to get another erection.

Claire smiled. "Oh my...."

He kissed her shoulder. "Believe me, this isn't usual. I had to be a teenager the last time I got it up this quickly this often. You should feel proud."

"What I am is turned on."

Dominic lifted her hair, trailing his tongue along her neck. "What do you want to do about it?"

Claire led him into the shower. She pushed him up against the wall and sank to her knees. She took him into her mouth, her fingers gripping his butt. His hands guided her head as water cascaded down her back. With a guttural groan, his third release came. He breathed deeply, tugging her back to her feet before they kissed long and deep, their tongues circling.

Eventually, they soaped each other and rinsed, dried off, and fell back onto the bed. Claire could have gone another round, but Dominic fell asleep, and Claire lay beside him, staring at him, smiling, one hundred percent ready, willing, and excited for this naughty little adventure.

As she finally closed her own eyes, a thought trickled in. What if this wasn't just some naughty little adventure? What if this was more?

———

When she woke, Dominic was gone. She checked the time, surprised to find it was four o'clock. The last time she'd slept through an afternoon she'd had the flu.

She rolled over, snuggling in and smelling the pillow where he'd been. Her top dresser drawer where she kept her bras, panties, and other various lingerie sat open. Dominic had been nosy. She should mind, but she didn't; she was more curious than anything.

Naked, Claire crossed the room. As she did, something on her windowsill caught her eye. He'd placed her vibrator on top of a blue satin negligee with a note that said simply: "10 PM."

He wanted her in the window tonight. Claire pressed her lips together, excited for whatever he had in mind.

Now dressed in a robe and down in the kitchen, she picked up her discarded clothes, did some light housework, and thought nonstop about later.

She took a bath, taking her time, enjoying a glass of wine and music. A text came in.

Fran: Well?????

Claire didn't respond. She wanted to keep this to herself for now.

Around nine she got ready, blow-drying her hair, putting on makeup, and dressing in the vibrant blue negligee.

A little before ten she stood in the window, seeing Dominic's dark room. Was he watching?

At exactly ten, he called.

"You look beautiful," he said.

"I want to see you."

"Not tonight."

"Tell me what you want."

"Put the vibrator in your mouth. Get it good and wet. Then bring yourself to climax. Don't hurry. Take your time. Make it last."

Softly, Claire gasped. Dominic ended the call.

Claire put the phone down. Slowly she licked the vibrator, moving her tongue up and down it, and taking it deep into her mouth. She lifted one leg, placing a foot on the windowsill, and she stared at his window as she slowly worked the vibrator over her clit.

She wanted him inside of her so badly.

Her breaths came heavy. She moved her negligee further up her thighs, gathering it around her waist, giving him a better view. Her hips moved slowly at first, taking her time, making it last. As he had instructed.

But it became too much. Her pace quickened. Her free hand came out, bracing herself on the window, her hips moving faster. And faster. And faster. Until the orgasm shot through her and she cried out, falling forward against the glass.

Her eyes closed, her chest rising and falling. She licked her lips. Eventually, she regained her equilibrium, and her foot that was still propped on the windowsill dropped limply to the floor.

She waited for Dominic to call or text, but nothing came.

On Sunday morning, Claire woke to the sound of a text coming in.

> Dominic: I'm making breakfast. Come over when you're ready.

Claire leaped from the bed. It didn't take her long to throw on fresh clothes, brush her teeth, and apply some light makeup.

She nearly ran from her house to his and she didn't have to knock because he opened the door as she trotted up his porch steps. He grabbed her and pulled her inside, pushing her up against the foyer wall and kissing her like a starved man.

"Good morning," he said, nibbling her neck.

"Good morning," she said, running her hands over his chest and around to grab his ass.

He pulled away, taking her hand and leading her into the kitchen. On the stove, he'd assembled scrambled eggs and sausage and had already sliced fresh strawberries onto two plates. As he served them both, Claire used the opportunity to glance around. Unlike her place with every room divided by walls and doors, his downstairs spread open and airy with one room bleeding into the next. She noted with pleasant surprise he'd completely unpacked and decorated it in masculine shades of cream and blue with burgundy colored furniture. For what she knew of him so far, it seemed suited.

"You ever been here before?" Dominic asked, leading her to the table in the nook of a window that looked out over his backyard and the trail beyond. Had he sat right here and watched her run? She hoped so.

"I have, yes."

He held her chair out for her in a very chivalrous way, helping her scoot into her spot. "Eat all of that. You're going to need the nourishment."

"For what?" Claire teased.

He gave a sexy little shrug. "This and that."

Claire couldn't wait.

Oscar's nails clicked on the hardwood floor as he wandered in to see who had arrived. Claire rubbed his head and Oscar lay at Dominic's feet.

Claire ate a bite of eggs. "What did you do yesterday after you left my place?"

"Errands. After all, I did have to buy condoms."

They shared a smile.

Dominic cut a bite of sausage. "What did you do?"

"Housework, took a bath, etcetera..." She didn't even think about buying condoms. Good thing he did. Claire sipped coffee. "You must have really wanted this house. The former owner said you made an offer they couldn't refuse."

"When I found out about the merger and that I was moving, I immediately started looking at neighborhoods. This house reminded me so much of the one I grew up in. I knew I had to have it. Honestly, I was surprised they took my offer."

"I'm glad they did."

Dominic fed her a strawberry.

Claire swallowed the bite, going back to her eggs. "Ever been married?"

"Are we getting to know each other, Claire?"

She felt a little stupid. "I suppose, but if you don't want to talk about yourself, just say."

"Mystery is sexier." Dominic offered that sensual half-smile.

All right, she'd go with it for now. After all, she'd only known him a week and this was exactly what she wanted—a wicked little rendezvous.

They ate, much like they had yesterday, staring at each other, not talking. By the end of breakfast, the erotic tension between them stretched so tightly that one small blink from either of them would snap it.

Dominic looked at her empty plate. "All done?"

Claire nodded.

"Now, I would like to fuck you into oblivion."

5

At work the next morning, Claire could not focus. She thought of all she had done over the weekend—all the ways she and Dominic pleasured each other, pleasured themselves while the other watched, all the positions, the toys, the restraints...

Sex with Brian had been good but tended to stay more vanilla than anything. Sex with Dominic, well... he welcomed and encouraged fantasy, exploration, and kink. She'd learned very quickly that he loved ordering her around.

Get down on all fours.
Moan loudly for me.
Suck it harder.
Open for me.
Tell me you like that.
Not yet. Wait.

He'd taken her to places she only imagined existed.

"Hello?" Fran waved a hand in front of her face. "Earth to Claire."

Claire snapped to, looking up at Fran. "Sorry."

"Oh my God, you did it, didn't you? With sexy neighbor?"

Claire's face heated. She nodded. "Fran, it was... I mean, there are no words."

Fran lowered herself into a chair. "Wow."

"Yeah."

"How many times?"

"A lot. Pretty much all day Saturday and Sunday."

Fran sighed. "I am so jealous."

"I can't stop thinking about it."

"I bet." She cringed. "But you better focus. You have a meeting in five minutes."

"I know." Claire gathered her things and hurried from the office. She took the stairs down one floor and walked into the conference room, already filled for the meeting. She chose a seat, nodding to the person sitting beside her, just as Dominic walked in.

She hadn't seen him since leaving his house last night.

He didn't glance her way as he sat across from her. The meeting began and she tried to pay attention, but her eyes kept drifting to Dominic, who still had not looked her way. Was he not affected like she was about their weekend together? One look at him and you'd never even know they'd been naked together.

After the meeting, Dominic exchanged pleasantries with a few people and then left the room, not even sparing Claire the tiniest glimpse.

It unsettled her. Why was he ignoring her?

Back in her office, she sat at her desk. Whatever euphoria she had earlier had completely dissipated. She didn't understand. What, he couldn't spare her even the tiniest of glances? It didn't make sense.

Her phone rang. Dominic's name lit up the screen. She

answered, hating how excitedly desperate her voice sounded. "Dominic, hi."

"Take off your panties and bring them to me. Now." He hung up.

Her first thought was, screw him and his order-her-around game. He couldn't ignore her and then just expect submission. Yet her pulse kicked in, fluttering with curiosity and renewed elation.

Her gaze darted to the open door where just beyond, Fran sat at her desk, typing on the computer. Claire reached under her dress, lifting up and sliding her red panties off. With them balled in her hand, she walked from her office past Fran's area and down the hall, her heart thudding heavier with each step.

Claire walked into Dominic's office where he sat waiting.

She handed him her panties and he maintained eye contact as he lifted them to his nose and inhaled. Claire's breath caught as he did. He tucked them away in his pocket, saying, "You haven't told anybody about us, have you?"

"No. Well, let me rephrase. Sort of. Fran knows I had a weekend with my neighbor but she doesn't know the neighbor is you."

"Not a word, Claire. This is just between us." He gave her that sensual half smile that she felt through her whole body, picked up a pen, and went back to work.

For several seconds, Claire stood in his office waiting for something. For another command, look, smile, invitation, anything... But nothing came.

So, she did the only thing she could. She turned around and left, the euphoria once again dissipating.

———

The rest of the day passed. Claire must have checked her phone a zillion times for a text or missed call but none came. She also walked by Dominic's office several times, hoping he'd glance up, but he never did. On her last pass by, she noted he'd gone for the day.

She didn't know what to think about the whole situation. She'd spent the most intimate weekend of her life with him and today he'd barely acknowledged her existence. Yet, wasn't that what she'd wanted? A no-strings, sexy fling? So, then, what was her issue? Dominic didn't owe her anything and office romances could get messy. But, my God, couldn't he at least spare her a look?

She felt irritated, mostly at herself. She needed to adopt whatever indifference he apparently had.

"What's up with you?" Fran asked as Claire packed her things for the day.

"Nothing. Why?"

"You're moody."

"Am I?"

"Um, yeah. It's very much not like you. After the weekend you had, I'd think you'd be in a better headspace."

Claire grabbed her briefcase and her purse. "Do me a favor and don't mention that weekend again, or the neighbor."

Fran blinked, taken aback.

Claire took her bad mood, walked past Fran, and left.

All the way home, Claire chastised herself. What was her problem? She was an independent, educated, mature woman and not some lovesick teenager who liked a boy more than he liked her. She went into this willingly and with both eyes wide open. She didn't want to play games though and would not give him the same cold shoulder that he was giving her.

By the time she turned onto her street, she'd decided to have a little talk with Dominic. If they intended to continue a sexual relationship, she needed kindness from him. He couldn't just ignore her and pretend she didn't exist. She did exist and she deserved respect. Otherwise, this would not work.

She was not expecting to find him playing basketball with Kelsey. Claire parked along the street and sat in her car for a moment just watching them laugh and have fun. He had a good laugh, one she would have loved to hear today.

In the grass lay Oscar, both eyes half closed as he watched them.

Kelsey grabbed the ball and dribbled, sending Claire a wave that she returned. Dominic smiled, motioning her to get out of the car. That smile flooded through her, lifting her mood. Maybe she'd misunderstood him today because, clearly, he was not ignoring her, otherwise he wouldn't be here right now playing basketball with her daughter.

Claire grabbed her work things and went to join them, smiling as Dominic dribbled a circle around her before doing a layup. Kelsey snatched the ball, bouncing it between her legs, and shooting a hoop. Dominic tossed the ball to Claire and she shot overhand, amazingly getting it in.

Dominic hooted, doing a silly dance that Claire and Kelsey both laughed at.

Yeah, she'd misread him earlier. He wasn't ignoring her; he was simply focused on work and not drawing attention to the two of them. Which, in hindsight, she appreciated. Rumors of a fling with Dominic was the last thing she needed circulating the office or getting back to the managing partners. She didn't think it would affect her possibly being offered the open senior position, but one never knew.

Dominic said, "I put a crock pot of chili on before I left for work. You two want to come over?"

"Sure!" Kelsey said.

Claire nodded. "Sounds nice."

———

Now dressed in a casual sundress, Claire sat beside Kelsey in Dominic's kitchen listening to the two of them talk about sports as they ate chili and cornbread. Friendliness filled the air much like when he came to their house for spaghetti.

They all chatted and laughed as the conversation drifted from topic to topic. It was all so…normal.

Kelsey asked, "Do you have children?"

Given that he'd stayed away from personal details thus far, Claire wondered if he'd answer or deflect.

"I don't," he said. "I always wanted kids though. Very much."

"You ever been married?" she asked next.

Normally, Claire would not encourage Kelsey to ask personal questions but she didn't correct her. Dominic seemed much more approachable with Kelsey around, and Claire did want to know more about him.

"I have. It didn't work out."

Kelsey quickly followed that with, "Would you get married again?"

"Maybe." He cut Claire a sideways look. "If I found 'the one,' I guess."

Claire's face heated. She looked away.

"Other than LinkedIn, you're not on social media,"

Kelsey said. "I looked."

"Correct." Dominic began taking the dishes to the sink. "And you shouldn't be either. Social media is a time suck and bad for your brain, not to mention privacy."

"But then how will I stalk the boy I like?" Kelsey joked.

"Like a normal stalker—follow him, watch him through his window." Dominic's words came lighthearted but they settled through Claire in an unsettling yet alluring way.

Kelsey put her bowl in the dishwasher. "Thank you for dinner. I have homework. I should probably—"

"Hold up." Dominic left the room and came back with two tiny keychain flashlights—one green and one purple. "As requested."

Kelsey eagerly took hers. "Thank you!" She flicked it on and off, smiling.

"You are very welcome." He put Claire's purple one on the table and went back to cleaning.

Kelsey gave Oscar a rub. "Like I said, homework. See ya later." With that, Kelsey left.

As soon as the door closed, Dominic crossed back over to the table and tugged Claire to her feet. He nuzzled her neck. "You and this dress are driving me nuts."

"Good, I was hoping it would." Claire tilted her head, giving his roaming lips full access. And even though she'd already reasoned things out, she still said, "Listen, I'm not very good at overlooking things. You ignored me at work today and it unsettled me. I wanted you to know."

He pulled back, taking a second to study her. "Claire, I'm sorry, I didn't mean to. I was trying to respect work boundaries. I guess I went a little overboard." Playfully, he pouted. "I'm sorry. I'll do better. Will you forgive me?"

A smile tugged at her lips. "Yes, I'll forgive you."

"Oh, goodie." He pecked her lips. "Now can we get on with things?"

"I suppose so," Claire teased.

Dominic led her from the kitchen, up the stairs, and into his room. He took his time with her, slowly undressing her, savoring every part, indulging in her. There was no hurry, no roughness, kink, or toys. No, Dominic Voss made love to Claire, and she forgot all about her emotional roller coaster of a day.

After, Claire enjoyed time just snuggling and soaking in the aftermath. Finally, she kissed him and padded into the bathroom to clean up. Back out in the room, she began to dress.

Dominic sat up. "What are you doing?"

"Getting dressed. What does it look like I'm doing?" she teased.

"Don't go."

"I have to get home to Kelsey."

"She's seventeen. She's fine."

Claire finished dressing. She went to him, kissing him again. "That's not how it works."

He grasped her arm. "Stay the night."

Her brow furrowed. "I...I can't."

For a few seconds, Dominic just stared at her through confused, sensitive eyes that gradually morphed into... anger? Why was he angry?

Throwing the covers aside, he climbed from the bed and charged across the room into the bathroom, slamming the door. Claire stood dumbfounded, listening to him run water and the bathroom drawers banging open and closed. She should've just walked out, but she sat on the edge of his bed and waited.

Eventually, the door opened and dressed in just boxers,

he glared. "I just shared the most intimate lovemaking of my life with you and you're leaving?"

Claire found herself without words. She struggled to comprehend just how irrationally upset he was.

"I told you things I've never told anybody!"

Claire searched her brain, coming up blank. What exactly had he told her—that he'd been married and wanted kids? Big deal, he'd told both her and Kelsey that.

"God, Claire, I never expected this out of you." He marched over to his dresser and pulled on a T-shirt and shorts. "Just go. It's what you want to do anyway."

But Claire didn't go. She honestly could not wrap her brain around this.

"And they say men can't get out of a bed quick enough. Well, you broke that myth. Glad I could be a reliable fuck." He slammed his dresser drawer closed.

Wow.

She continued sitting, watching him, trying to compose her thoughts. He stood with his back to her, breathing heavily.

Claire wanted to leave, but she found herself going to him instead. Calmly, she placed a hand on his shoulder, and her voice came gentle. "I'm sorry, Dominic. I didn't mean to make you feel as if your emotions don't count. I certainly didn't mean to reduce you to a reliable orgasm in bed. I truly enjoyed our lovemaking." She ran a hand across his shoulders. "Will you forgive me?"

She didn't miss the fact that she was apologizing to him for exactly what he had done to her earlier that day.

His shoulders rose and fell on a deep breath. He turned to her, tears in his eyes, and hugged her tight, burying his face from view. Claire hugged him back, both bewildered and touched by the level of emotion coming from him and also...a little frightened.

If she hugged him long enough, he'd be okay and she could leave. At least that's what she told herself.

Some time later and with his head still buried in her neck, he softly asked, "Will you stay with me?"

No, she wanted to say but the word failed to come from her lips. She'd never done this before—stayed over with a man and left Kelsey alone. She didn't know what to do and certainly didn't want a repeat of his anger. Despite her best judgment, she said, "Let me just text Kelsey."

He kissed her passionately. "Thank you, Claire. Thank you."

She kissed him back—going through the motions—wondering how she could do such a one-eighty in the span of a day. She'd gone from desiring one look, one touch, to now wanting nothing more than to get away from this man.

6

Claire did not sleep. She spent the night wrapped tightly in Dominic's arms, listening to him breathe. Early the next morning, she managed to extricate herself from him and went home before Kelsey woke. Opting not to run, Claire closed the blinds tightly in her room and got ready for work.

She was just about to go downstairs when Kelsey's words came back to her. *Other than LinkedIn, you're not on social media.*

With her phone, Claire googled, "Dominic Voss, Nashville, TN," seeing the profile that Kelsey had. Claire clicked on it and an image of his handsome face filled the screen followed by a write up of everything she already knew from the merger.

Down the hall, Kelsey's shower kicked on. Claire put her phone down and went to the kitchen. She busied herself making her daughter's favorite—a ham, feta cheese, and tomato omelet with dill.

Sometime later and dressed for school, Kelsey came into the kitchen, holding Louie, her hamster. She stood at the threshold, her confused gaze bouncing from Claire to the omelet and back to Claire.

"Good morning!" Claire said, a bit too brightly.

"It's not my birthday. In fact, it's *your* birthday tomorrow."

"I know. Can't a mother do something nice for her daughter?"

Kelsey hid a smile as she sat at the kitchen island. "You're either in a good mood because Dominic rocked your world or you're faking it out of guilt."

Claire chuckled, but it had no humor in it. "Guilt." She served up the omelet. "I'm so sorry, Kelsey."

"All good." In her lap, Kelsey made a nest out of a kitchen towel and Louie snuggled in.

"No, it's not. It won't happen again."

Kelsey took her first bite of the omelet. "I'm glad you're dating."

"Thank you, but it's the one thing I promised you and myself—to be here every night that you are." Claire poured her daughter a mug of coffee. "I am truly sorry."

"You're being harder on yourself than you should be. Mr. Voss seems like a nice man. Plus, you were just next door. If I needed you, I knew where you were. I'm seventeen, Mom. I was fine."

"Thank you for saying all of that, but still."

Kelsey kept eating. Claire sipped her coffee and began making herself some scrambled eggs.

The front door opened. "Girls?" Brian called out.

"Kitchen!" Claire called back, surprised. She hadn't realized Brian was coming over this morning.

Dressed for work, he appeared, smiling. But Claire knew that smile—it was his fake one.

"Have you eaten?" she asked.

Brian shook his head. "I'll take eggs too if you're in the mood."

"I'm in the mood."

While Brian served himself coffee and sat beside Kelsey, Claire busied herself cracking more eggs.

Brian snagged a tomato from Kelsey's plate. "You excited for later? First game of the season."

"Beyond excited. Want me to save your usual bleacher spot?"

"You know it." Brian petted Louie as he surveyed Claire. "We meeting there or should I pick you up?"

"Let's meet there. I'll leave from work."

"We're doing our usual after, right?" Kelsey asked.

Claire and Brian exchanged a smile. It was their family ritual for all the first games—if Kelsey lost, they went for conciliation frozen yogurt and if she won, they did a gigantic and very greasy pepperoni and sausage pizza that Kelsey always ate the majority of.

"Standing ritual. We wouldn't miss it." Brian snagged a chunk of feta off his daughter's plate.

Claire served both of them scrambled eggs. Outside a horn honked. Kelsey crammed one last bite in. "That'll be June." She put Louie and his towel on the counter and jumped up. "Will you all put Louie up?"

With a nod, Claire waved her off as Kelsey snagged her backpack and basketball duffel, gave Louie a little kiss, and ran out the door.

"I think we have the only teenager who would rather be chauffeured around than own her own car," Brian said, smiling.

Claire returned the smile, taking Kelsey's seat and eating her first bit of eggs. "Speaking of, if she doesn't come around on the car thing, we're going to have to think about another graduation gift."

"Well, we've got the year. We'll figure it out."

They ate in comfortable silence, Brian finishing his eggs first. He wiped his mouth and took his and Kelsey's plates to the sink. "Your big four-oh tomorrow. What do you think?"

"I think there better not be forty candles on my cake."

Brian laughed as he began loading the dishwasher and cleaning the skillet. Claire ate the last few bites of her eggs and sipped more coffee, watching him. It had always been so comfortable with Brian. That's why she felt at ease saying, "It won't happen again."

"I figured you knew why I was here. Listen, I called Kelsey last night. She mentioned you were staying over with Dominic. She didn't specifically call to tell me."

"I didn't think otherwise."

Brian placed the skillet on the drying rack and then began wiping counters. "We both know the rules. We made those rules. Not even with Laurie did I break them."

Laurie had been a serious two-year relationship for Brian that ended about six months ago. "I know," Claire said.

"It's not like you."

Claire sighed, fiddling with her mug, looking everywhere in the kitchen but at Brian.

He placed the rag over the faucet to dry and looked at her, waiting patiently for Claire to meet his eyes. When she finally did, she saw compassion…and concern. "Anything you want to talk about?"

"No, but I promise, it won't happen again. I know our rules. I'm truly sorry and I did apologize to Kelsey."

"Okay. Enough said. Want me to put Louie up?"

"Nah, I got him."

Brian came around the counter and kissed her on the cheek. "See you later for the game."

"Yep, later." She continued sitting, listening to him leave.

Seconds later, her phone beeped with a reminder that Habitat for Humanity was due any second. Good, she couldn't wait to finally have her garage available to park in. She picked Louie and her dishes up, moving around the island to the sink. She placed Louie on the windowsill and began washing her things. As she did, she glanced past Louie and out the bank of windows that gave a view of the backyard and trail.

There stood Dominic, with Oscar, staring right into her house.

The doorbell rang. Claire jumped, dropping her mug, and it shattered in the sink, nicking her finger. She quickly wrapped a towel around the blood and went to let in Habitat for Humanity.

———

Claire didn't usually close her office door unless she was in a meeting but she closed it today, telling Fran, "I need to focus. I'm behind big time. Unless it's an emergency I want to be left alone."

Fran gave her an odd look.

Claire sighed. "I'm sorry. I'm not trying to be a—"

"Bitch?"

"Yes. I've just got a lot going on."

"Anything you want to talk about?"

Claire gave her a quick hug. "No, but thank you."

"Okay, get on in there and work. I'll man things out

here." Fran closed the door.

Thankfully, focus came easily and Claire lost track of time as she sifted through documents and checked things off of her to-do list. She felt the concentration in her neck and back and realized she hadn't been out of her chair in hours. She stood and stretched. She'd placed her phone on silent and used the opportunity to check her messages, finding several from Dominic.

> Dominic: I didn't like waking up and finding you gone.
>
> Dominic: Why is your door closed?
>
> Dominic: I saw your ex at your house this morning.
>
> Dominic: Your secretary said you don't want to be disturbed.
>
> Dominic: Are you ignoring me?
>
> Dominic: Claire?

She reread each text, getting more anxious as she did. She could ignore him and dive back into work or she could address the issue. She texted him back.

> Claire: Can you come to my office?

His response came immediately.

> Dominic: Yes.

Claire opened the door. "Mr. Voss is on his way."

"You want lunch?" Fran asked. "I'm headed to Chipotle."

"Sounds good. Get me that chicken bowl thing I like."

Dominic rounded the corner, coming to an abrupt stop when he saw Claire. An odd silence filled the space. Fran hesitantly looked between them. Claire stepped aside, motioning him in and as she began to close the door, she looked at Fran who mouthed, *What's going on?* But Claire shook her head, closing the door.

Dominic had already taken a seat and Claire sat behind her desk. She looked at his face, not seeing the handsome features, only the man.

"Are you breaking up with me?" he asked.

Were we dating? She wanted to respond but refrained. Instead, she clasped her hands on top of her desk and leveled him with a patient but also serious look.

"Dominic, I think you're an intelligent, handsome, hardworking man with a great sense of humor. I have thoroughly enjoyed our time together outside of work, but it has gotten way too intense too quickly. I am a mother before anything else in my life. I am upset with myself for not being with Kelsey last night. I should have never bent to your request and frankly, you should have never insisted. I broke my own rule." Claire picked her phone up, showing him the screen. "These texts? Too much. I'm going to be blunt. It is none of your business that Brian was at my house this morning. He is Kelsey's father and we have a wonderful relationship that I greatly value. I also did not like looking out my kitchen window and seeing you standing there staring in. It unsettled me."

She stopped talking, allowing the space for him to respond. But he didn't. No, Dominic took his time digesting her words, maintaining eye contact as he did. She searched his expression, trying to get a read on his thoughts, but he kept a poker face in check.

Eventually, he spoke. "You women are all the same. The

moment a man shows you any real attention or emotion you're done."

"That's not true."

"Oh yeah? Well, you were fine playing the kinky fuck game. Then it all changed last night when I opened up. Okay, fine. We can go back to meeting in the window every night and getting our rocks off."

Claire took a persevering breath. This was not going as she had hoped.

Dominic shoved back from the desk and stood. He paced the small area—back and forth—not looking at her. Then he stopped, something shifting in his expression, gentling, almost pleading. "How about we start over? Let's go on an official date. What do you say?"

This time yesterday Claire would've jumped at that offer but too much had happened in too short a time. "Thank you but I think it's best if we just be neighbors and co-workers." Claire stood. "I hope you understand."

She walked around her desk in the opposite direction he stood and opened the door. Claire didn't look at Dominic as she waited for him to leave. Thankfully, he did without another word.

The rest of the day passed uneventfully. Claire didn't see Dominic once. She met Brian at Kelsey's game and after, they took the winning girl for pizza. By the time Claire pulled into her newly empty garage, she felt back to normal.

She'd done the right thing ending things with Dominic.

―――

Turning forty felt like turning thirty-nine, or thirty-eight, or thirty-seven... No big deal. Claire woke early and dressed in running clothes. With a light attached to her head, she hit the trail before the sun came out. She'd missed the last couple of training days and made up for it today with fifteen miles at an easy ten-minute pace.

Over two hours later, she rounded the last curve and slowed her pace. Though the sun had already risen, she'd forgotten to turn her headlamp off and did that now. Her breathing came steady—in through her nose and out slowly through her mouth. Her heart rate slowed. Sweat slicked her skin, and she wiped her face with the hem of her tank top.

With her hands on her hips, she paced the trail in front of her house, breathing, allowing her pulse to continue slowing. As she did, her gaze slanted over to Dominic's home. She didn't see him, but she knew he was up and getting ready for the day. If she lingered any longer she might run into him walking Oscar.

That thought had her trotting across her backyard and into her home.

Kelsey greeted her with a glass of water and a silly dance. "'Go shawty, it's your birthday. We gon' party like it's your birthday. And we gon' sip Bacardi like it's your birthday.'"

Claire laughed. "I'd squeeze you but I'm disgusting."

"I don't care!" Kelsey threw her arms around Claire. "Happy forty, Mommy!"

Claire's heart squeezed with love. She couldn't remember the last time Kelsey called her 'Mommy.'

Kelsey clapped her hands. "Okay, go get clean and I'll make your favorite breakfast."

Upstairs, Claire did just that, smiling, excited for the day.

Some thirty minutes later, she walked into the kitchen

finding Kelsey had already served up pecan- cranberry pancakes drizzled in melted peanut butter. Claire eagerly sat and dove in, telling herself the fifteen miles deserved this high-caloric breakfast.

"Okay, so the plan is we rally back here after work and school for junk food, carrot cake, and back-to-back rom-coms," Kelsey said. "Assuming that's still what you want to do?"

"Absolutely."

"In the junk food department, I'm guessing Arby's curly fries and beef and cheddar?"

"You know me too well."

"Dad's bringing the carrot cake, minus the forty candles."

Claire grinned. "Sounds perfect."

"I'm also doing popcorn and M&Ms. We will all be in a proper food coma."

Claire playfully pointed her finger. "And no presents. I'm serious."

Kelsey crossed her heart as she began cleaning.

At work, Fran had decorated Claire's office like a five-year-old's birthday with multicolored balloons, streamers, a giant "Happy Birthday" banner, and the telltale black ribbon she insisted Claire wear across her body bearing the words, "Forty: It's all downhill from here."

Stuffed from breakfast, Claire opted for no lunch but she joined Fran in the breakroom while she ate hers.

"You seem normal today," Fran said, digging into her sushi. "It makes me happy."

A little bit of Claire's good joy dimmed. She hated she'd been so off with Fran. "I'm sorry. It's been a weird few days."

"I love you. All good." They toasted with green tea. "Too

bad it's not sake. Listen, I know you've got your thing with Brian and Kelsey but let's go out this weekend and martini toast your big day."

"Deal."

"And don't forget at three you're supposed to go to the conference room for a 'surprise' birthday cake."

Claire laughed. "Got it."

———

At three she arrived to a joyful and collective "Happy Birthday!" from almost everyone in the firm. A large sheet cake had been decorated with a giant 40 candle. A couple of people cut and served up the cake and they all sang her "Happy Birthday."

Claire noted with relief Dominic's absence from the celebration.

Later, back at home and dressed in yoga pants and a baggy tee, she settled down with Brian and Kelsey in the living room. On the coffee table, a spread had been assembled of Arby's, cake, popcorn, and way too many other things Kelsey had decided to add.

The three opted to watch *Bridesmaids* first.

An hour in and belly extended, Claire reclined on the sofa, her feet up, nibbling one last bite of carrot cake when the doorbell rang. Kelsey jumped up and Claire put the movie on pause.

She listened to Kelsey open the front door. "Hi!" she said. "Come on in. We're in the living room."

Seconds later, Kelsey preceded Dominic. Cautiously, Claire sat up.

Dominic extended a beautiful hand-tied collection of wildflowers. "I heard there's a birthday girl in the house."

Claire accepted the gift, carefully eyeing him. "Thank you."

Dominic offered Brian a friendly look. "Good to see you again."

"You too." Brian got up from the couch, indicating Dominic should sit. "Join us."

"Oh, that's okay." Dominic gave Claire a genuine and very normal smile. "I just wanted to stop by real quick."

"Stay," Kelsey insisted. "We have entirely too much food. Help us eat it."

Dominic chuckled as he surveyed the containers and wrappers covering the coffee table. "You three are going to be miserable tomorrow."

"Seriously stay," Kelsey said. "Right, Mom?"

"Of course," Claire responded, still feeling cautious but also a little okay with it. He just seemed so back to himself—smiling, laughing, personable. Perhaps a day to think through things made him see things from Claire's point of view and to cool off some.

Plus, she felt safe with Brian and Kelsey nearby.

Dominic chose to sit in a recliner as Claire took the flowers into the kitchen and put them in a vase next to an enormous bouquet her mom had sent. When Claire returned to the living room, Dominic and Brian were laughing at something while Kelsey cut him a piece of cake.

Claire took her spot back on the couch next to Brian, and Kelsey spread out on the floor. For the next hour, they watched the rom-com, laughing. Every once in a while Claire would slant a look Dominic's way to find him comfortably reclined, a slight smile curling his lips, amused by the movie.

Whatever tendrils of wariness clung to Claire slowly unraveled as she fully relaxed, enjoying the time. She'd made the right decision talking to him. He did seem okay and very back to normal.

A text came in on her phone.

> Mom: I know you're doing your thing with Brian and Kelsey and you didn't want presents and blah blah blah…but Happy Birthday my sweet girl. I can't believe my baby is 40!

Grinning, Claire texted her back.

> Claire: I love you, Mom, thank you! I'll stop by soon for a visit. And the flowers are lovely. You did not have to do that!

Her mom sent her a kissy emoji followed by a dancing birthday cake that Claire giggled at.

Another text came in, this one from Matt, her blind date.

> Matt: I heard from Fran that it's your birthday today. Just wanted to say Happy Birthday!

> Claire: Thank you!

> Matt: I'm on a big project right now but maybe after it wraps we can get together for that do over date?

> Claire: Sounds good.

Grin still in place, Claire put her phone down and went back to the movie.

She didn't notice that Dominic had been watching her.

7

The next morning Claire walked into her office to find a single white rose with a small envelope attached to it on her desktop. She lifted the flower, inhaling, as Fran poked her head in.

"Belated birthday present, I guess. It was there when I came in this morning." Fran bopped her brows. "Secret admirer?"

"Doubt it." Claire put her things down and opened the envelope, pulling out a card. Silently she read, *Please give me another chance.*

"Well?" Fran prodded.

"You're right. Belated birthday." Claire put the card in her purse and the single rose in a mug, using her water bottle to give it a drink.

She settled behind her desk as Fran began going through scheduling calendars, prep for upcoming meetings, and other deadlines and status reports.

Once Fran left, Claire sat for a bit, idly staring at the rose and revisiting the card. Last night things did seem back to normal with Dominic. Had she overreacted earlier?

She picked up her phone and sent him a text.

> Claire: Thank you for the rose.

> Dominic: Glad you liked it. I promise to be better. No intensity. No possessiveness. Your daughter comes first. I get it. What do you think?

Intense and possessive—apt words for sure.

She took a second, thinking again of how normal he seemed last night. Then she texted him back.

> Claire: Okay. Yes. Let's try again.

Proceed with caution, Claire told herself.

> Dominic: Dinner out tonight?

She checked her calendar.

> Claire: That works. Kelsey is spending the night with her dad.

They exchanged a few more texts with a time and place and then Claire put her phone down, delighted to feel excitement, and got to work.

At six that night, Claire walked into the steak house they had decided on. The hostess saw her to their reserved table where Dominic waited sharply dressed in a linen sport coat and button down shirt. Claire maintained eye contact with him as she walked through the restaurant, pleased to feel those familiar flutters and that alluring sensual pull.

He stood, kissing her on the cheek and holding her chair

out. Dominic had already ordered a bottle of cabernet and poured them both a glass.

He lifted his for a toast. "To trying again."

With a smile, Claire clinked glasses and sipped. She'd been to this restaurant before and though they were known for their steaks, their salmon far exceeded any she'd ever had. She placed her order for the cedar planked fish and Dominic chose prime rib.

"Cabernet with salmon?" he asked. "You want to change to white?"

She waved that off. "I don't care about that stuff."

Their Caesar salads came and they both began to eat.

"Thank you for last night," he said. "That was fun, hanging out with you all. I've never seen *Bridesmaids* before."

"It's a modern classic. I've seen it several times. What was your favorite scene?"

"Any scene with Melissa McCarthy."

Claire laughed. "Oh good, she's my favorite."

A couple of women settled into the table beside them, both giving Dominic an interested once-over that he didn't even register. Claire did, though, sitting up a bit, feeling herself swell. Dominic was a good-looking man who only had eyes for Claire.

He leaned in, surveying her salad. "You're not eating the croutons."

"Not a fan. Want them?"

"For sure." He lifted his plate and she scraped her croutons over.

They continued eating. Claire asked, "Did you come straight here from work?"

"I did. Why?"

"What about Oscar?"

Dominic gave her an odd look. "You didn't know I hired Kelsey?"

"No... she didn't tell me," Claire said, finding that peculiar. She remembered Kelsey offering, but her daughter never mentioned anything after that.

"Yeah, I already knew she was spending the night with Brian. He took her to my house to feed and walk Oscar." He showed her his phone and their text exchanges.

> Kelsey: Since you're going out with Mom tonight, should I take Oscar with me to Dad's?

> Dominic: No, that's okay. He'll be fine until I get home. Just feed and walk him.

> Kelsey: Dad's picking me up from practice after school. I'll have him take me to your place.

> Dominic: Sounds good, thanks.

Claire scrolled up, reading their exchanges that dated back to last week when they first met, including the night Claire stayed over with Dominic and Kelsey inviting him to their place last night. It unsettled Claire that Kelsey and Dominic had been texting and neither had thought to tell Claire.

"What?" Dominic said, taking his phone back.

"Why didn't you tell me you were texting with my daughter?"

Dominic shrugged. "I didn't think it was a big deal."

Claire put her fork down, nudging the salad away. Dominic did the same. The waiter came and took their plates. Claire and Dominic silently stared at each other as the waiter returned with their main dishes. He put their plates down, glancing between them, as they continued holding each other's gaze. Tension stretched, filling the space.

"Does everything look in order?" The waiter hesitantly asked, to which neither responded. "Well, just let me know if you need anything." He walked off.

Just then, Claire's phone received a text.

> Brian: I know you're on a date with Dominic and please don't freak, but Kelsey needs stitches. I'm taking her to the ER now.

Claire began to grab her things. She was just about to tell Dominic why she was leaving when he reached across the table and grasped her forearm.

"What are you doing?" he demanded.

The harsh tone made Claire pause. She looked at his fingers on her arm and then up into his face.

His grip tightened. "Is this because I've been texting with Kelsey? You're overreacting. Chill the fuck out."

Her words came steady and perfunctory. "Let go of my arm."

Dominic did not; instead, his grip tightened.

"You had no business exchanging all those messages with Kelsey. Especially the other night. How dare you tell her I was sleeping over at your house. It's not your place. It's also not your place to tell her we're on a date tonight. *I* didn't even tell her that."

His jaw tightened. "Who texted you just now? Brian?"

Despite his fingers digging into her arm, Claire stood. He kept his grip in check as he, too, stood. It was then that Claire noted the attention they'd drawn from the women sitting beside them and others nearby but she kept her gaze level and steady with his.

"This was a mistake," she said. "Release me. Now."

The waiter cautiously approached. "Is everything okay here?"

Dominic's fingers slowly, stiffly, released her. His fury-filled eyes transitioned to calmly meet the waiter's gaze. "Everything is fine. The lady is leaving."

Claire turned and walked from the restaurant, ignoring the hushed comments and concerned stares.

What the hell was she thinking, agreeing to dinner with him? Dominic wasn't "back to normal," whatever that even meant. Claire wasn't sure he *had* a normal. She was not overreacting and she most certainly did not need to "chill the fuck out."

———

At the ER, Claire rushed in to find Brian holding Kelsey's left hand as a nurse wrapped gauze around her right index finger.

Claire pressed a kiss to her daughter's head. "What happened?"

"Mom, you didn't have to leave your date for this."

"What happened?" Claire repeated.

"She was cutting an apple and sliced right through her index finger," Brian said. "Six stitches later and we're all done. You missed all the fun."

Kelsey made a face. "The doc says no basketball for a week."

Claire kissed her again. "You'll live."

"Kelsey's right," Brian said. "You didn't have to leave Dominic for this. I had it handled."

Claire kept her mouth shut, choosing instead to plaster a smile and change topics. "Seeing as how this is your first ever ER visit, that deserves lots of pampering. I am at your disposal." Claire bowed. "Your every wish is my command."

Brian laughed, bowing too. "Same goes."

Kelsey giggled. "Boy, this is going to be fun. I guess we'll start with ice cream."

Later, after going out for ice cream, Kelsey opted to go home with Claire versus spending the night at Brian's. Claire got her settled in bed and a painkiller down her. As Kelsey snuggled into her linens, Claire sat on the bed's edge, stroking her daughter's hair, watching her eyes grow heavy. Tomorrow they needed to talk about Dominic. Claire did not want her to exchange messages with him anymore or take care of Oscar, but she would need to choose her words carefully.

Kelsey drifted fully into sleep. As Claire was just about to turn out her bedside light, a text from Dominic lit up her daughter's phone. Claire keyed in her unlock code.

> Dominic: You okay? Are you in a lot of pain?

Claire scrolled back up, reading the messages before that.

> Kelsey: Dad just texted Mom. Sorry to ruin your date :(

> Dominic: Yes, Claire left. Much to my dismay. Guess I'm eating alone…

> Kelsey: I cut myself and need stitches. Dad's driving me right now to the ER.

> Dominic: Tell your mom I'm sorry.

> Kelsey: What did you do?

> Dominic: Just tell her that.

> Kelsey: OK

> Dominic: BTW, how are you texting with a cut finger?

> Kelsey: Voice to text ;)

Claire deleted the string and then deleted Dominic's contact information. She also blocked him from Kelsey's phone. When she got to her own bedroom, she texted Dominic.

> Claire: I deleted your name from my daughter's phone. Do not make contact with her again. Find another dog walker.

Then like with Kelsey, Claire deleted the text string and his name and blocked him from her own phone. First thing tomorrow she would talk to Kelsey.

In the morning, Claire walked into the kitchen to find Kelsey sitting at the island eating cereal and exchanging texts.

"How's my patient?" Claire asked.

Kelsey dramatically poked her bottom lip out and stuck her index finger in the air. "I'm very pathetic."

Claire laughed. "Do we need to amputate?"

"Maybe..."

Claire got coffee while Kelsey went back to texting.

"Is that June?" Claire asked.

Kelsey chuckled as she read the latest message. "No, Mr. Voss."

Claire froze. What in the hell?

"Weird enough, he disappeared from my phone. But luckily he texted me this morning, giving me his new number so all is good. By the way, he said he was sorry. He didn't tell me why. Still, he wanted me to tell you that. What'd he do? Is he in the doghouse?" Her phone buzzed again.

Kelsey was just about to check it when Claire said, "Will you put that away? We need to talk."

"Oh-kay." Kelsey put her phone down, giving her the side eye. "What's up?"

Claire took a deep breath, carefully choosing her words. "Mr. Voss and I are not going to see each other anymore. Given that, I'm not comfortable with you seeing him either."

"What? *Why?!* He's a nice man."

"I'm not going to go into details. Just know he did a few things that made me uncomfortable. I've already told him I don't want him communicating with you anymore and that he needs to find a different dog walker."

"Mom," Kelsey whined. "Please don't do this."

Claire held strong. "The fact he's still in contact with you despite my request makes me very upset."

Kelsey's eyes narrowed. "You deleted him from my phone, didn't you?"

"I did, last night when you went to sleep. Kelsey, why didn't you tell me the two of you were exchanging so many text messages?"

"I don't know. I guess I thought you knew, that maybe Mr. Voss told you. I'm sorry. I didn't purposefully hide it. Is *that* what this is about? Is that why he apologized to you and that I can't talk to him anymore?"

"Partly, but there is more to it than that. I need you to hear me and to tell me you understand that I do not want you communicating with him. It stops now." Claire held her gaze steady, waiting on her daughter.

The thing about Kelsey, she wore her emotions, and Claire watched the myriad cross her face—bummed, confused, irritated, and finally resigned. "Fine, whatever. Can I go?"

"Yes, you can go."

Kelsey took her phone, left half a bowl of cereal, and went upstairs to finish getting ready for school.

Years ago when Kelsey first got a phone, Claire and Brian monitored it via an app to make sure Kelsey was being responsible, but mostly to give them peace of mind that some sex predator wasn't preying on their daughter. As expected, Kelsey treated the phone sensibly and Claire and Brian no longer felt the need to monitor her daily texts and whatever else.

It had been four years since Claire last launched the app. She trusted Kelsey to follow her instructions but Claire did not trust Dominic. With a sigh, she reactivated the app. It was better to be safe than sorry. Hopefully if her daughter found out, she'd understand it was for her *own* protection.

―――

On the way to work, Claire dialed Brian.

"How's our girl?" he asked.

"I told her we might need to amputate."

Brian laughed.

"Listen," Claire said, "I do want to talk to you about something..."

The conversation after that went well. Claire opted not to go into great detail but enough was relayed that he understood Dominic Voss was not welcome in their home or to be around Kelsey anymore.

―――

That night at their favorite Mediterranean place, Claire and Fran sat a high top table, a few sips into their Friday night belated birthday martinis. Emboldened, Fran said, "I have been dying for an update on the sexy neighbor. Spill. And don't spare the details."

Claire jokingly rolled her eyes. "Fizzled and died." She shrugged. "It was fun while it lasted."

Fran heaved a bummed sigh, clinking her martini glass rim to Claire's. "Here's to your vagina seeing some action that will hopefully get it through to the next adventure."

Right then, Dominic walked in and strolled past without seeing them. He made his way over to the packed bar, sidling up to a beautiful Latina in a slinky red dress that hugged her every curve, complemented by black stilettos.

She'd already ordered him what looked like a whiskey on the rocks and Dominic sat on the stool beside her, his back to Claire. He and the woman toasted and sipped. They talked, their bodies a respectful distance—at first—moving closer as the moments ticked by.

Beside Claire, Fran was saying something but Claire remained fixated on Dominic as he leaned in, whispering in the woman's ear. She offered a sexy smile in return.

"Hello?" Fran said.

"Sorry," Claire mumbled still watching.

Dominic and the woman didn't make it through their drinks. He paid. They stood, and with his hand on her lower back, he led her from the bar.

He didn't glance in Claire's direction once.

"Was that Dominic Voss?" Fran asked.

Claire's throat felt dry. She cleared it, nodding.

"Lord, that man is hot."

Claire sipped her martini, a bit unsettled but also... relieved that he'd redirected his focus onto someone else. She swiped her phone, checking the app that monitored Kelsey's cell use. As expected, her daughter had done as asked with the last text being:

> Kelsey: Mr. Voss, I won't be able to help you with Oscar anymore. Thank you.

To that, Dominic had not responded and Kelsey deleted any remaining messages lingering in her phone.

Good girl.

At home later, Claire checked on Kelsey who, despite it being Friday night, was doing homework in the living room. Satisfied, Claire went on up to her bedroom. Post martini, it would be an early night for her. She started closing the room's blinds, and then stopped.

Across the way, Dominic's blinds were not only open but up with all the lights on, giving a very graphic display of him and the Latina from the bar having rough sex up against the wall. Claire watched his naked ass pound into the woman, who gripped his hips with her thighs, still wearing the black stilettos. Then with the woman's head thrown back in ecstasy, Dominic carried her from the wall to the bed.

With an unsteady hand, Claire closed the blinds.

Dominic purposefully did that, knowing she would see. Did he also orchestrate the meetup at the bar knowing Claire would be there? She wasn't a paranoid person, but her mind still went there. If this was some sick game, she didn't want anything to do with it.

Fuel to the fire. Claire believed in that. If she ignored him long enough, he would stop.

8

On Saturday, Brian manned the grill while Claire and Kelsey hung out on the back deck, sipping lemonade and chatting.

"You excited about the marathon?" Brian asked, checking the steak.

"More nervous, I think."

Kelsey kicked her feet up on the railing. "You've been training consistently. You got this."

Brian closed the lid on the grill and drank from his bottle of beer. "Are you hoping to place or just survive?"

"Survive." Claire laughed.

"You did a half marathon before." Brian joined them at the outdoor table. "I remember when you crossed the finish line you told me you could have run ten miles more."

"True," Claire agreed. "Let's hope I feel that way tomorrow."

Kelsey swiped a baby carrot through hummus. "Aren't you supposed to carb load? Shouldn't we be eating a giant pot of spaghetti?"

"Nah." Claire waved that off as the wind changed directions and she got a whiff of the steak. Her stomach growled.

Oscar lumbered up onto the deck, going straight to Kelsey. Sitting with her back to Dominic's house, Claire stiffened.

"Oh my gosh!" Kelsey gave Oscar a good rub. "Hi, buddy." She kissed his head. "What are you doing over here?"

Brian glanced past Claire where a shadow shifted as Dominic walked up the two steps to their deck. "Sorry about that." He didn't look at anybody as he clipped a leash onto Oscar's collar and led him back down, across their backyard, and onto the trail where he slowly and casually strolled away.

The outside air grew stagnant. Uncomfortable silence smothered the deck.

Brian and Kelsey both looked at Claire who looked anywhere but at them. She'd given them sparse details and knew they were curious but Dominic was her issue, not theirs, and she had it handled.

Eventually, Brian got up and went back to the grill. Kelsey took her phone out of her pocket and began scrolling. And Claire just sat there drinking lemonade and hating that she'd ruined their perfectly lovely Saturday afternoon.

Bright and early Sunday morning, Claire checked in for the marathon, soon affixing her assigned number to her tee and joining the throng of runners pulsing forward. She kept her pace even, averaging an eleven-minute mile, and some six hours later, crossed the finish line where Brian and Kelsey stood beside each other, loudly cheering.

After sweaty hugs were exchanged, Brian handed her an electrolyte drink and energy bar, and Claire took her place in line to receive her finisher's medal.

The line moved quickly, Claire sipping her drink, eating her bar, and moving forward until just one more person stood between her and the volunteer giving out medals. The person in front of her received his, moving away, yet Claire stayed right where she was, staring at the person working the booth.

Dominic Voss.

His indifferent gaze met hers, touching down to the number affixed to her chest, before finding it on a spreadsheet and checking it off. He selected a medal from the table situated between them and held it out. But still Claire didn't move.

The person behind her nudged her, and Claire finally stepped forward, a bite of unchewed bar in her mouth. Not even a flicker of recognition crossed Dominic's expression as she took the medal from him. Then he looked right past her to the next person in line and Claire moved around the booth and back over to where Brian and Kelsey waited.

As the three of them walked through the crowd, heading to their cars, Claire chanced a glance back at Dominic who remained busy checking off and handing out medals.

Again, Claire wasn't a paranoid person, but she was becoming one. Like Dominic's appearance at the bar, Claire wondered if he was taunting her.

———

On Monday morning, Claire strolled into her office to find a small gift wrapped box on her desk with no card attached.

Fran entered, two coffee mugs in hand, and a thick file under one arm. She put a mug down for Claire followed by the file. "That's the Lewis information. Just a reminder, they're coming in tomorrow." Fran nodded to the box. "That was there when I got in. Another belated birthday gift?"

With a shrug, Claire untied the ribbon and wedged the lid off, immediately putting it right back on.

Fran frowned. "What is it?"

Angry, embarrassed heat crept into Claire's cheeks. She fisted the box and charged past Fran. "I'll be back." She strode down the hall and straight into Dominic's office, closing his door and tossing the box onto his desk. "That's not funny."

He leaned back in his chair, a tight smile in place. "It wasn't meant to be funny. I simply thought you'd want your panties back."

Claire's jaw clenched. "I thought we weren't going to let this affect our work."

"Did we say that?"

She glared.

"You started it when you brought me your panties."

Claire saw red. "Are you following me?" she demanded.

His dark brows came up. "Come again?"

"Friday night you just happened to be at the same bar as me. Saturday, you conveniently let Oscar wander up onto my deck. And Sunday you were at my marathon. It's a little too coincidental, Dominic. Not to mention the show you put on Friday night in your bedroom with that woman."

The tight smile stayed in place. "Don't flatter yourself, Claire. I'm not following you. My hookup picked that bar herself. Oscar saw Kelsey and wanted to say hi. And as far as Sunday, I volunteered for that race before we stopped seeing each other as a show of support. And regarding my Friday night bedroom 'show?' Perhaps you need to stop being such a creepy voyeur."

Creepy voyeur. She didn't like that he used the same words she'd thought of her own self.

She snatched back the box and got right in his face. "Stay away from me. I'm serious."

He held his hands up, the tight smile now becoming smug—an odd combination with his suddenly vacant gaze.

Claire turned away, wanting to slam his office door behind her, but made herself take a deep breath instead. The last thing she needed was office gossip.

Outside his office stood Fran, a concerned look on her face. "What's going on?"

"Nothing," Claire gritted, passing her by and heading down the hall.

Shit. Shit. Shit.

She'd been kidding herself. She did not have this handled.

———

Evening runs weren't really her thing, and Claire needed to give her body a rest after the marathon, but pent-up energy drove her from her house and down to the trail. She didn't bother warming up, she launched into a full-on run, her feet pounding the mulched trail. She had no mileage or time in mind; she simply needed her heart to pulse and for sweat to drip.

In the back of her mind, one tiny smidgen of doubt niggled around. Maybe Dominic *had* coincidentally been at the same bar as her. Maybe he had volunteered for the marathon out of support. Maybe Oscar did really just want to say hi to Kelsey. But the sex show and the returned panties were definitely calculated moves. And then there was that smug smile of his, the indifferent gaze, the fearsome grip he had on her forearm at the restaurant, and the demanding jealous tone to his voice. Plus the text exchanges with her daughter even after Claire requested that he stop.

Oh, yeah, he knew exactly what he was doing. Worse, it worked. Dominic had riled her up.

Claire's pace quickened. Night fell. She turned on her headlamp.

She thought of their first weekend together and how eager she'd been to please him, completely submissive to his dominating demands. She recalled how cold Dominic treated her at work after that weekend. Then, almost like a flip of a switch, he became needy, begging her to stay. Then another flipped switch when she saw through his "give me another chance" note.

God, if she could rewind the clock she would, but she couldn't. All she could do was move forward. Except she knew in every fiber of her being that this Dominic problem was not going away.

Her pace slowed to a jog. Sweat soaked her clothes in a satisfactory way. She paced the trail near her home. Her gaze shifted, piercing through the night, fixing on Dominic's house. She'd never worried about neighborhood safety at night or running on this trail. She did now though. She'd put herself in a vulnerable position out there alone.

She couldn't see him but she felt him staring—or perhaps she imagined it—either way, and vulnerable or not, she flipped him off. Then she charged across her yard and into the house. She needed to get ahead of this; she just wasn't sure how.

―――

The next morning with a purse over one shoulder and a soft leather briefcase gripped lightly in her hand, Claire walked the hall toward her office. She rounded the corner and came to an abrupt halt. There was Dominic, one hip propped on Fran's desk, his arms folded, as the two of them shared a laugh.

Fran caught sight of Claire and waved. "Good morning!"

Claire's eyes met his. The green depths danced with humor as his laughter smoothed out to a retained smile. "We were just talking about you," he said, all light and friendly.

"Oh?" Claire responded, flatly.

"I was telling him about that time a few years back when you tripped going into a meeting and almost broke your nose. Do you remember that? You had tissue crammed up your nostril and blood on your blouse but you were full speed ahead in the meeting." Fran laughed. "God, you are something else."

Claire kept her tone even as she maintained eye contact with Dominic. "Did you need something?"

Still smiling, Dominic stood. "Nope. I like Fran. I stopped by to say hi." With that, he gave a little good-natured wave to her executive assistant and walked off.

Claire looked at Fran, whose expression dimmed. "I'm sorry. I don't know what's going on between the two of you, but—"

"Doesn't matter. I need a meeting with HR." With that, Claire went into her office.

Where Fran normally came in for a morning chat, she remained noticeably at her desk. Claire sat and put stuff away. She reached for the Lewis file she'd left out last night, ready to dive back in, when she noted it gone.

She looked through the piles on her desk, then her briefcase before moving over to the filing cabinet. Moments later she walked to Fran. "I left the Lewis information on my desk last night. Have you seen it?"

"No."

"The meeting's today. I need that file."

Fran got up. "Let me look."

While Fran proceeded to search everywhere Claire already did, Claire nervously paced. She was absolutely sure that she left those documents front and center, knowing it would be her first task of the day. "Do you think the cleaning crew accidentally moved it?" she asked.

"Of course not," Fran said. "They never touch anything unless it's in a garbage or a recycle bin."

"How much of the file do you have scanned?" Claire asked.

"Roughly half. I was waiting for you to finish before I did the rest."

"Shit," Claire hissed, watching Fran close the last drawer on the filing cabinet. "Okay, send me what you scanned, get us both coffee and come into my office. We have to recreate everything before the meeting."

Fran nodded and got to work.

Claire was just about to sit back at her desk when a thought trickled in...

Did Dominic have anything to do with this?

Claire and Fran worked tightly for hours recreating the lost file. The client meeting went off perfectly. Claire didn't know if Dominic had been the catalyst or not, but starting today, she would lock her office door every night. Security had never been an issue before but Claire would not take any more chances.

At the end of the day, she had a conversation with Human Resources.

"Thank you for seeing me," Claire said. "I know there are no specific rules about office dating, but I wanted to let you know that Dominic Voss and I had a brief relationship that has ended." There, at least it would be officially documented—by Claire—should any more of his games bleed over into work.

The HR Director merely nodded, responding professionally, "We'll follow protocol and note your file."

"Is that it then?"

"Unless there's an issue, there's nothing else. Mr. Voss already came to us as well. We appreciate both of your professionalism."

Claire's eyes narrowed. "When was this?"

"Last week."

"Did he...say anything else?"

"No. Just what you did."

"Thank you." Claire kept her composure as she walked from HR, gathered her things, locked her office, and left the building.

She wanted to scream, and as soon as she was in her Lexus, she would. She walked briskly to her car, her pace slowing as she caught sight of her very flat, back tire. "Mother of God," she mumbled.

"That sucks." Fran came up beside her. "I'll call Triple A."

While Fran did that, Claire looked around the parking lot for Dominic's black BMW, but it was already gone. This was an old building with no security cameras. If he had anything to do with the tire, there was no way to prove it.

Thirty minutes later, roadside assistance arrived. They surveyed her tire, pointing out a black embedded nail. Did Claire run over that? Could be, but she highly doubted it.

With the tire fixed, Claire drove home. Tomorrow she would install security cameras on her house, her car, *and* her office. If she was being paranoid, fine, but if not, she would catch Dominic in the act. Then she would take the proof to the cops and have him arrested. For the first time all day, Claire felt empowered and she took what seemed like the first real breath in hours.

That's when the phone calls began.

Over Bluetooth, her cell rang. She didn't recognize the number, but it was the local area code, so she answered, thinking it might be a client. "Hello, this is Claire Quade."

Silence.

"Hello?"

The call clicked off.

Seconds later, the same number called again. "Hello, this is Claire."

Silence.

"Hello?"

The call clicked off.

Seconds later, again. This time Claire didn't answer. It rolled to voicemail. Whoever it was did not leave a message.

Minutes later a different number popped up. Claire gave it a chance. "Hello, this is Claire."

Silence.

"Hello?"

The call clicked off.

Seconds later, it rang again. Claire did not answer.

Minutes ticked by. Another call, this one from yet a different number.

Claire did not answer.

Minutes ticked by. Another call, this one from yet another number.

Claire did not answer.

Her thirty-minute commute home continued, the calls coming in every few minutes from different numbers. She let them all roll to voice mail. No one left messages.

At home, she pulled into her garage and cut the engine. On her phone, she blocked every single number that had called her—fifteen in all.

Throughout the night, the calls continued. No matter how many she blocked, another came in.

In her room, she opened the blinds and glared at Dominic's house. But no lights were on. She imagined him over there, sitting in the dark, calling her over and over again on however many burner phones he'd bought or from some app that did this sort of thing.

Eventually, the calls stopped.

She went to bed but she didn't sleep. She stared at her ceiling. Whatever empowerment she felt earlier slowly drained as she feared whatever he planned next.

9

The next day, an exhausted Claire stood in the kitchen blearily watching Kelsey buzz around making them both coffee and peanut butter toast. Well, at least one of them got some sleep.

Kelsey handed Claire a mug, surveying her eyes. "No offense, but you look like shit. Are you sick?"

"Didn't sleep." Claire slid onto a barstool and eagerly sipped the strong roast.

Two slices of Ezekial bread popped up from the toaster. Kelsey placed one piece on a plate. "You want a little or a lot?"

"A lot." Claire yawned.

Kelsey liberally coated Claire's toast and gave it to her.

"You are the bestest daughter in the entire world."

"Yeah, yeah, yeah."

While Claire ate, Kelsey got her own serving ready and took the stool beside Claire. But before she could take her first bite, Kelsey's phone lit up with a call. She checked the number and answered. "Hello?"

Silence.

"Hello?"

The call clicked off.

Claire's gaze slid to Kelsey's phone. Dread settled in.

Kelsey took a bite of her toast. Her phone rang again. She checked the number, answering, "Hello?"

Silence.

"Who is this?"

The call clicked off.

Claire took her daughter's phone and blocked the number.

A few seconds later, it rang yet again. Kelsey checked the number. "It's this area code."

Claire once again took her phone, blocking that number as well. Then she turned Kelsey's phone off. Her daughter slid her an inquisitive look.

"Same thing happened to me last night—over and over and over again. I'm getting us both new numbers today." She held Kelsey's phone up. "You'll be okay without this for one day?"

"Yep, all good." Kelsey sipped her coffee. "Stupid marketing calls."

Claire said nothing.

To use Kelsey's term, it was time for Claire to go from playing defense to offense.

———

As Claire drove to work, she called a security company, arranging for a home system to be installed as soon as possible. They told her Friday—two days from now—was their first opening. She agreed and scheduled things. Then she called the Lexus dealership about having a car cam installed. She made that appointment for tomorrow—Thursday.

A mile from work, she pulled into an Office Depot and bought a nanny cam. At work, she closed her door and placed the nanny cam in a potted plant that took up one corner of her office. She followed the instructions, downloaded the app, and had it connected within fifteen minutes.

If Dominic came anywhere near her car, home, or office, she'd catch him.

Finally, she sat, closing her eyes, the weariness of no sleep pulling at her. She could not believe this was her life. She'd always led a drama free, safe existence. She and Brian had picked the neighborhood she lived in for its school district and its family environment. It was supposed to be a benign area where children could play in the yards, things like security systems weren't needed, and neighbors could be counted on.

She'd brought this on herself. For the first time ever Claire had decided to do something outside of her comfort zone and it had come back to bite her in the ass. She regretted every second of Dominic. But all she could do now was get security in place and hopefully record him doing something suspect. Then she'd turn the evidence over to the cops and let them handle him.

With a stifled yawn, Claire keyed her password into her workstation and was just about to begin returning emails when Fran knocked on her door before cracking it open. "Dominic Voss wants to see you."

Claire didn't look up. "I'm busy."

Dominic pushed past Fran like he had every right to be in Claire's office. Completely drained, she shrugged. "Whatever."

Fran gave her a worried look, stated, "I'll be outside if you need me," and then closed the door.

Dominic made himself comfortable in Claire's guest chair, crossing his legs, delivering a cocky expression that had no impact on her. In fact, she ignored him as she went back to the emails, beginning a reply to the first one.

He sat quietly, watching her.

Fine, let him sit there all day. She didn't care. She refused to give him the satisfaction of a response.

Minutes ticked by.

Claire kept working.

Finally, he spoke. "I am in love with you, and all you seem capable of is injuring my heart."

In love? He barely knew her.

"I would do anything for you," Dominic continued. "Anything. Don't you understand that?"

Claire kept working.

"Hell, Claire, I'd go to the end of the world for you and back."

She wished he would—go that is and never come back.

"I can't believe you've whittled our love to this." Dominic waved his hand between them.

Claire yawned.

"I have never felt this way about any woman before."

Sounded like a personal problem to her.

"I was ready to propose."

Claire kept stoically working, though it was increasingly difficult to maintain focus due to the utter absurdity of his words.

"Is that what you want? Is that what I did wrong? I'll drop to my knee right now."

Claire hit enter and started the last sentence of her email.

"I would be a hell of a better father to Kelsey than Brian could ever be. I would happily give you another baby. We would make a beautiful baby. You know we would."

Claire clicked send on that email and launched into another.

For several minutes Dominic said nothing.

Claire moved her mouse, selecting and attaching a file.

He surged to his feet. "You're a fucking cunt," he snarled under his breath before flinging open her door and charging out.

Claire kept typing.

Fran instantly reappeared but before she could say anything, Claire spoke first, her tone tired just like she felt. "If you could just close my door, I'd really appreciate it. I need to be alone."

Fran didn't immediately do as requested.

Claire made eye contact with her, offering an exhausted smile. "Please?" she softly said.

Fran studied her for a long second, then with one single nod, she left Claire alone.

For several long minutes, Claire sat, staring at nothing particular, a small satisfied smile gradually curling through her lips. Good, let *him* be riled up for a change.

She got her phone and brought up the nanny cam footage of what just happened. But... nothing came through. No video and no audio.

"Dammit."

She double-checked she'd set it up correctly and tested it several times. Everything seemed to be working correctly. Dammit. Dammit. Dammit. What the hell?

Fine. She may not have got him this time, but she would the next.

The rest of the day came and went with no more drama.

Thankfully, Fran didn't press the issue but Claire knew she was going to have to tell Fran everything. Just not today. Instead, Claire packed up her things, took hers and Kelsey's phones to the store, and got both of them two new numbers.

On the way home she dialed Brian.

"Hello?" he answered.

"Hey, it's me. Kelsey and I both have new numbers. This is mine. I'll have Kelsey text or call you when I get home from hers."

"Okay...why?"

"We were both getting a lot of prank, hang up calls. I got tired of blocking all the numbers."

Silence. Then, "That's weird. Because I've been getting similar calls all day long."

Claire briefly closed her eyes. Son of a bitch.

"Guess I'll change mine too," Brian said.

"Probably a good idea. Let me know when you get your new number."

———

That night Claire sat in bed, her laptop balanced on her lap. Brian was with Kelsey in her room, discussing a paper for school. Every once in a while their voices or laughter floated down the hall, eliciting a smile. But it had been a while since she heard them, so she figured they were deep into research.

As was she.

Claire brought up Dominic's LinkedIn profile, once again perusing it. Though Kelsey said—and he confirmed—that he wasn't on social media Claire still typed his name into Facebook and Instagram. Nothing popped up.

She redirected, keying in just his last name with Nashville, and this time a Facebook profile appeared for Vanessa Voss. Set to private, Claire saw only a photo of the iconic Nashville Printer's Row. Claire pulled up a new tab, searching "Vanessa Voss, Nashville," and in return received an address. Nothing else.

Claire went back over to Facebook and requested they be friends with the message: "I recently met Dominic Voss. Any relation?"

She clicked "send" right as a knock sounded on her open door, and Claire looked up to see Brian. An unexpected calmness settled through her, and she took a deep and relaxing breath. It was the first soothing one she'd taken all day.

With a serene and welcoming smile, she closed her laptop and set it aside, holding her hand out to him. Brian's lips curved in an equally tranquil way. He crossed her room, taking her hand, sitting on the side of her bed.

She wanted to tell him everything, but she didn't. She feared Brian would confront Dominic and things would quickly spiral and escalate from there. No, she did feel confident she could handle this without involving Brian.

So, she kept quiet, and in the dim light, she continued breathing calmly, taking in the contours of Brian's adorable, comforting face. She was catapulted back to when they met in college and how they did everything together—eating, homework, school events, hanging out in each other's dorm rooms. They were inseparable best friends.

Despite moving things into intimacy, the unexpected pregnancy, and the marriage they both knew was based more on their alliance than love, Claire always knew their deep friendship would take them into old age. Brian had been and would always be the one constant in Claire's life. The one person she could count on.

Perhaps it was the roller coaster of emotion she'd been on, or the memories, or the fatigue of no sleep, but Claire leaned forward and tenderly kissed Brian. There was no pause from him, no surprise; it was like he knew what she needed as he cupped her face and sweetly returned the kiss.

"Kelsey go to bed?" Claire whispered.

Brian nodded.

"Close the door."

As Brian did, Claire began to undress. Brian joined her, stripping from his jeans and tee. He gently, warmly, came down on top of her, stretching out, filling her soul with coziness. They made slow love, exploring each other's bodies, taking their time, giving the other much needed comfort, love, and intimacy. To Claire, it was both familiar and new; it had been years since they'd shared a bed.

When things finished, Brian kissed her gently and Claire rolled over, urging him to spoon her and stay. She slept well, wrapped in his devoted arms, feeling his warm breath on her neck and listening to his deep and easy sleep.

She'd missed this. She'd missed him.

When morning dawned, Claire and Brian were both already awake, neither speaking, and neither ready to get up when Kelsey softly knocked. Still spooned in front, Claire glanced over her shoulder at Brian who nodded his go ahead.

Claire snuggled back into her pillow. "Come in," she said.

Kelsey opened the door, freezing in place, her surprised gaze bouncing between them.

Claire smiled. "Good morning."

Kelsey full-on grinned. "This is cool."

Brian chuckled.

"Why don't you give us some privacy and we'll meet you downstairs," Claire said.

"Okay." Still with her grin, Kelsey left, closing the door.

They continued laying, not moving, enjoying the quiet moments. Claire welcomed the blessed noiselessness in her brain.

Eventually, Brian slid from the linens, padding into the bathroom where Claire joined him for the morning routine. She gave him a new toothbrush and as they did their teeth, they stared at each other in the mirror, both smiling like last night had been their first time and not their umpteenth.

Brian rinsed his mouth and spat. Naked, he folded his arms and propped his hip on the counter. "Well, how are we going to explain this to our daughter?"

Also naked, Claire pressed a kiss to his cheek. "If you don't mind, I'll handle it. Trust me?"

"I absolutely trust you." He started the shower and stepped in. Claire joined him.

There was no intimacy, just the two of them cleansing and getting ready for the day, both back to being best friends and sometimes lovers.

Later, Claire stood on the front stoop waving as Brian left for home before work, driving right past Dominic who was out walking Oscar. Leash in hand, Dominic's piercing gaze trailed after Brian and just as he turned to scowl at Claire, she gave him her back and went inside the house.

She found Kelsey in the kitchen. Once coffee and oatmeal were made, they sat beside each other at the island. They'd talked about sex a lot over the years. Thankfully, Kelsey felt comfortable coming to her mother with questions, and Claire always answered with honesty.

That was why Claire felt relaxed launching right in. "I know you haven't had sex yet but one day all of what I'm about to say will make sense. That is unless you have had sex and you haven't told me...?"

"Nope."

Claire nodded. "Sometimes when you have sex it's slow and loving, other times it's fast. Sometimes it's for your partner, and other times it's for you. As you know, the first time I had sex I was your age and it was with a boy I had a crush on. It was sweet and awkward and a memory I think fondly of. We ended up dating about a year after that. The second boy I had sex with was a mistake. I was in college at a party with too much alcohol. It was a one-time thing and never happened again. The third boy was much like the first —very sweet—and we ended up dating for six months. The fourth was your father who was and still is my best friend. After we divorced, I did have a few encounters here and there but nothing significant. Then came Dominic. I'm telling you all of this because sex means different things. Last night your father and I both needed and wanted each other. It was in no way a mistake. It also doesn't mean we are getting back together. We're a family and will always be a family. I didn't want you to think it meant we were getting remarried or he was moving in or anything else. I didn't want there to be confusion."

Claire paused, giving Kelsey time to absorb everything just said.

"Okay," Kelsey smiled. "Thanks for explaining. I get it."

"Good."

The two went back to their oatmeal and coffee. They were almost done when Kelsey said, "Was Mr. Voss a sweet encounter or a mistake?"

"Mr. Voss was most definitely a mistake."

10

Claire left early from work. She drove her car to the dealership where they installed the dash cam and showed her how it worked.

While she waited to check out, she texted her mom.

> Claire: Forgot to tell you that I'm coming to visit today. I already blocked off my calendar. You better be there!

> Mom: LOL, Fran already told me. Can't wait!

As Claire was checking out at the dealership, the receptionist caught sight of the tiny purple flashlight on Claire's keychain. "That's neat. Is that a flashlight? Where did you get that?"

Claire took it off and handed it over. "Here, all yours." She never wanted to see the thing again.

From there, she drove to her mother's retirement community. Situated on Lookout Mountain, the fifty-five-plus active adult municipal featured lakefront homes, a clubhouse, shopping, golf, rolling mountain vistas, exercise facilities, lap pools, pickleball, and daily social activities. Claire's mom prided herself on being a young seventy-year-old woman and had a busier social calendar than Claire, Brian, and Kelsey combined.

Being single, Claire's mom opted for a small one-bedroom condo instead of a sprawling house. Claire parked her Lexus in the semi-full lot, choosing a spot with no one on either side. With her purse looped over her shoulder, she walked into the three-story building made up of only fifty units and took the elevator up to the third floor.

Her mom's corner unit sat at the end and it didn't take Claire long to walk the tiled hallway. She owned a key to the place but out of respect, she always rang the doorbell.

She waited for her mom to answer, staring out the decorative window that offered a view of the golf course, busy with afternoon players.

The door opened. With a smile, Claire turned...

And froze.

There stood Dominic, smiling broadly. "Claire! Come in."

Her mom appeared beside him. "Claire, you naughty girl. Why didn't you tell me you were dating such a handsome and friendly man?" She pulled Claire in for a quick hug. "Come in. Come in. I was just making us coffee."

Claire stiffly walked past Dominic and into her mom's condo. Dominic made himself at home in the femininely decorated living room, sitting on the blush striped couch and kicking his shoes up on the matching ottoman. Carrying an ornate silver tray with a carafe and fancy porcelain tea cups, her mom came from the kitchen into the living room. She placed the tray on the coffee table and went about pouring each of them a cup.

"How do you take your coffee?" she asked Dominic.

"Cream, please," he said, that broad smile still in place.

Claire rigidly sat on the edge of a padded, pastel green chair, staring speechlessly at Dominic.

Her mom gave him his cup, fixed Claire's, and then with her own coffee in hand, she relaxed on the couch. With a sweet expression, she looked between them. "You two make the cutest couple." She sipped.

"Thank you!" Dominic enthusiastically responded.

Claire's fingers tightened around the delicate cup.

Dominic tried his coffee, peering at Claire over the rim. "Put your purse down. Make yourself comfortable."

"Yes," Claire's mom agreed. "Relax. You look stressed."

"How long have you been here?" Claire asked, hating to hear tightness in her tone.

"Not long," Dominic said, still with that stupid smile. "I saw you took the afternoon off and decided to as well."

Like all things on Claire's personal agenda, Fran had blocked this visit off in Claire's Teams calendar. How did Dominic see it and know she'd be here? Did he hack her computer? Or he could have just looked at Fran's monitor. She always had Claire's calendar up on her screen.

"Isn't that sweet? How kind of you two to come visit me today," her mom said, so incredibly clueless. "Anyway, Dominic was just telling me how you met. He said he's new to the firm, saw you at an office party, and fell instantly 'in like.' Then imagine his surprise when he bought a house right beside you." Her mom laughed. "It was meant to be!"

Dominic toasted the air with his tiny cup. "That it was."

Still with her purse over her shoulder, Claire put her coffee back on the tray. She pretended to check her phone. "Mom, thank you for the coffee but Dominic and I need to leave. I just got a message there's an emergency back at the office."

Her mom pouted. "Oh, that just bums me out. Are you sure?"

"I'm sure." Claire stood. She gave Dominic a pointed look.

With that shitty smile still in place, Dominic placed his cup on the tray. "Tell you what, we'll come back."

Her mom's face lit up. "Promise?"

"Promise." Dominic got to his feet, nobly holding his hand out to help her mom up. He gave her a warm goodbye hug. "So delightful to meet you, *Mom*."

Claire's teeth ground. Her mother giggled.

She saw them to the door, standing there, watching them walk away with Claire in front and Dominic just a step behind. At the elevator, Claire jabbed the button. The door opened, and they stepped inside. Claire's mom still stood watching and Claire offered a forced smile. Dominic grinned and waved.

The elevator slid closed, and Claire whirled on him. "You *son of a bitch*. How dare you!"

Dominic's grin vanished. He slammed his hand on the "stop" button and pushed Claire up against the wall. He pressed his body to hers, grinding against her, latching onto her neck and sucking hard.

Yeah, well, she'd taken self-defense with Fran.

With all Claire's strength she shoved him off of her and lunged for the button right as he smashed into her again. He spun her face-first against the elevator wall, and aggressively groped her breasts, her butt, her thighs. He yanked the hem of her dress up and was just about to push his fingers into her panties when she head butted him.

He stumbled back, dazed.

Claire lunged once again for the button, punching it hard. The elevator started again. Claire made a fist and punched him right in the throat. He gagged. She kneed him in the balls. With a loud shout, he crumbled forward.

Claire got her dress back in order just as the elevator door opened. She ran out and across the lobby and was just about to dial nine-one-one when Dominic staggered through the open elevator door.

"You don't want to do that," he sneered, placing a thumb drive on the tiled floor before walking gingerly out the other side of the lobby. Claire crossed over, watching him through the windows as Dominic made his way to the furthest parking spot, got into his BMW, and pulled from the rear lot.

Dread settled through Claire as she went to retrieve the thumb drive.

Robotically she walked from her mom's condo building, out the front, and over to her car. Her hands trembled as she beeped open her Lexus, got the air conditioning running, and retrieved her laptop from its soft case.

What seemed like an eternity ticked by while she waited for her laptop to boot. Her hand continued to tremble as she put the flash drive in. A window popped up filled with jpeg and mp4 files.

She barely breathed as she selected the first one. An image filled the screen of Claire dressed in lingerie standing in her window, her foot up on the sill, masturbating for Dominic.

She clicked on the next image—her giving him a blowjob.

The next—her on all fours while he pounded into her from behind.

The next—her handcuffed, legs graphically splayed as she seductively stared into the camera.

Another—her blindfolded.

Then a video—her licking chocolate from his chest.

Another video—her moaning and arching while he went down on her.

Another—her on top, her hips pumping hard to orgasm.

Image after image...video after video... all highlighting Claire with his sounds muted and his face artfully hidden. Except for the masturbating in her window, they were all taken in his room by concealed cameras. Pictures and videos that displayed her at her most private and vulnerable moments.

There was no note but she received the message loud and clear.

He would not hesitate to send this to everyone at the office, to Brian and Kelsey, to Claire's mom. Hell, he would not blink an eye at uploading them to the internet.

Dominic would release them if Claire didn't keep quiet and do exactly what he wanted.

———

Darkness fell as Claire drove to Fran's house. She called Brian on the way.

"Hi," his voice cheerfully greeted her.

It sent a pang through her heart.

"Hey, I'm running later than I thought. Can you keep Kelsey tonight? I'm not sure when I'm getting home."

"No problem. I'm actually hanging out with her right now. We're at your place playing a rousing game of HORSE."

"She's not supposed to be playing basketball."

"She's fine. Her finger's nearly healed. Don't worry, I'm keeping an eye on her. She's mostly shooting with her left hand which is good for me. I might just win the game."

Tears pressed Claire's eyes. She loved her family so much. God, what a mess she'd made. She sniffed and cleared her throat.

"You okay?"

"Hi, Mom!" Kelsey yelled.

"I'm fine." Claire focused on having a normal voice. "Hi!" she called back and Brian relayed the greeting.

"Want me to just stay here for the night?" he asked.

NO! was the response she wanted to scream. She didn't want them anywhere near Dominic. "Actually..." A sudden thought crept in. "I was hoping we could temporarily move in with you. I've been seeing roaches and then just yesterday—and don't tell Kelsey this—I found a family of rats in our attic," she lied.

"Yikes."

"I know. Anyway, I called an exterminator and they're coming after the weekend. They may have to tent the place."

"Oh, wow. Yeah, of course. I'll have Kelsey pack a couple of week's worth of clothes. Want me to pack for you?"

"No, I'll pack and then meet you all at your place. Tell Kelsey about the roaches but, of course, keep the rats under wraps."

"Okay, see you later."

They hung up, and Claire breathed deeply. Her family would be safe.

Not too much longer, she pulled up in front of Fran's house, noting her car parked in the driveway and her husband's truck gone. Good.

She knocked on Fran's door.

Seconds later it opened and Fran blinked in surprise.

"I need a friend," Claire said, tears clogging her eyes.

Now seated in Fran's cozy living room with two glasses of merlot, Fran curiously studied Claire who fidgeted with the glass, feeling nauseated.

Fran clasped her hand. "We've got all night. Sean doesn't have to work tomorrow so he went to visit his dad in Georgia." Fran squeezed Claire's fingers. "Take your time."

Claire's hand trembled as she drank a healthy portion of the merlot. She placed the glass down, tightly interlocking her fingers, inhaling shaky breaths. She felt tears again and pressed the palms of her hands to her eyes. Her voice quivered when she said, "I'm in big trouble, Fran."

Fran placed her wine beside Claire's and wrapped her in a warm hug that made Claire give in to the emotion and tears.

Sometime later, Claire got herself in check. She blew her nose, drank more wine, and started talking. "The neighbor I told you about is Dominic Voss. What I thought was going to be a fun, adventurous, sexy interlude has turned into a nightmare. Most recently, hours ago, he physically assaulted me in the elevator at my mom's condo. He has pornographic images and videos of me that he plans to release if I don't 'behave,' I guess. He's threatened me multiple times now. He follows me. He anonymously harassed Brian and Kelsey. He took that file from my office and flattened my tire. I can't prove any of it, though. I've tried. I even set up a nanny cam in my office but it ended up not recording. It wouldn't surprise me if he had something to do with that as well. He's sneaky and manipulative. Possessive. And underneath it all, he continues to proclaim his undying love and devotion for me. He even proposed marriage."

Claire paused, her voice cracking with more tears. "Fran, I don't know what to do."

"Everything makes so much more sense now," Fran said. "I knew something was off. You have been acting so strange. My God, Claire."

"I'm sorry," Claire whispered.

"No, don't do that."

"He's devious. He puts on that friendly, handsome smile and everyone just clicks into place. He knows exactly what he's doing. He's seasoned at this, I can tell. He's too good at the manipulation game. He's premeditated. He installed cameras in his bedroom for God's sake! There's no telling how many women he's done this to…" As Claire said that last part, she thought of Vanessa Voss in Nashville. "I found a Vanessa Voss in Nashville. I don't know how they're related but maybe she's got information. I messaged her on Facebook but she didn't respond."

"We're going to Nashville," Fran stated. "This weekend. We'll take my car. You can tell Brian it's business." Fran sat back thinking. "You said Dominic assaulted you in the elevator. There might be a camera."

Claire shook her head. "There's a camera on the front of the building, but nothing else."

"What about tomorrow? I saw you have an appointment with a home security company."

"Yes, to install a system. I made it for nine in the morning knowing Dominic would already be gone for work." Claire let out a humorless laugh. "Who am I kidding? He knew I'd be at Mom's. I'm sure he already knows about the security system too. It probably gave him a good laugh."

"Doesn't matter. Follow through with that. Go to work and then come here. You can stay the night and then we'll get up early Saturday morning and drive to Nashville."

Claire stared at Fran's fierce face, feeling hope begin to blossom and also relief that Claire had someone to help her carry this burden. She pulled Fran into a tight hug. "I love you so much. Thank you."

Fran pushed to her feet. "This asshole is going down. He's picked the wrong two bitches to mess with."

They said goodbye, and Claire drove the thirty minutes home. As she pulled into her garage, she noted Dominic's house was completely dark. He could be in there right now watching her. There was no way to tell and so she worked quickly, packing suitcases.

She also packed her gun.

She hadn't even thought of the gun in years. It was something her mom and her had done together. They went to a range, did a week's long course, and both received concealed weapon's licenses. Truthfully, Claire had done it for her mom whose good friend had been mugged and it scared her to death. Claire wanted her mom to feel safe and at the time apparently owning a gun accomplished that, so Claire happily attended the course.

Now, she felt happy to have.

In the privacy of her garage she put everything in her trunk and made fast work of leaving the neighborhood. She kept one eye on the rearview but saw only intermittent nightly traffic and no tail.

Not many minutes later she arrived at Brian's place. After their divorce he'd bought a townhouse only a few miles from the home they'd shared as a family. The proximity made things easy.

He must have been watching for her because he came straight out to help her move things in. Claire wasted no time starting with yet another lie. "Looks like I have to go to Nashville this weekend on business. I'm leaving after work tomorrow. You'll be okay with Kelsey?"

"Of course."

Brian put her luggage in the primary suite. "All right, I'll leave you to it. There's leftover chicken if you're hungry."

Food was the absolute last thing on her mind, but she knew she needed to eat—even though she had been feeling a bit nauseated. "How about toast?" she asked.

"With butter?"

Claire nodded. That did sound good. "Oh, and by the way..." Here came yet another lie. "I heard there was a break-in a few houses down, so I decided to get a security system. It's getting installed tomorrow. Once I learn how to work it, I'll show you and Kelsey."

"Between rats in your attic, roaches, and now possible burglars, our sleepy little neighborhood isn't so sleepy anymore."

"Yeah." Claire chuckled, trying to sound indifferently lighthearted but it came out more forced than anything.

Brian eyed her just long enough that Claire had to turn away. "Toast?" she reminded him.

Thankfully, he left and Claire went straight into a long hot shower.

Later, with Kelsey in her room and Brian on the living room couch, Claire lay in Brian's bed. She did not sleep, she stared at the unmoving ceiling fan listening to the air conditioning kick on every fifteen minutes or so.

Her mind raced.

Claire prided herself on being a strong and independent woman who knew how to handle her own problems. It had taken her years to learn that part of that strength came from knowing when to lean on someone else. It was okay to ask for help. The person she'd always leaned on was Brian, but Claire wanted her family as far from this as possible.

So then why was she there? It only put both of them at risk.

11

Friday morning she met the security company at her house. It didn't take long to install cameras and an alarm. After that, she went to work. At the end of the day, she drove to Fran's and spent the night.

Saturday morning, they began the two-hour drive to Nashville.

Sitting in the passenger seat, Claire stared out the window, watching trees go by. "Dominic will soon figure out I'm not at home. It won't take him long to deduce I'm staying at Brian's." Through her sunglasses, Claire glanced at Fran, her thoughts from last night trickling in.

"What are you thinking? Do you want to stay with me?"

"I need to move into a hotel. I'll tell Brian and Kelsey I'm out of town on work."

"I think you need to remove yourself from work altogether. You have plenty of leave built up. Just take it."

"I can't do that, not with the possible promotion around the corner." Possible promotion... she hadn't thought about that in days. And to think that had been her primary focus for the past several months. Now all she could think about was the lunatic terrorizing her life and how to stop him.

"Tell them it's a family emergency."

Claire thought through that. "You're right. I'll go in on Monday, we'll get my schedule figured out, and I'll put in for immediate leave. I'll tell HR just that—family emergency."

"Perfect. Plus, it'll drive Dominic nuts that you're not there." Fran cut Claire a sneaky grin.

Yes, Claire liked this idea. It would give her distance from her family while she dealt with all of this Dominic Voss shit.

Some two hours later the GPS led them through a historical area lined with brownstones where Vanessa Voss lived. Hers sat midway, made of red brick and towering three stories. Claire and Fran found a parking spot a few blocks away and walked side by side down the quaint street.

As they neared Vanessa's brownstone, an unsettling eeriness began to move through Claire and she stopped walking.

"What is it?" Fran asked.

"I don't know. Just give me a second." Claire looked up and down the street, spying an elderly lady behind them standing on her stoop gardening in a white planter's box. Claire backtracked, and Fran followed. "Excuse me?" Claire said to the lady.

She glanced up, a sweet smile on her face. "Yes?"

Claire pointed to Vanessa Voss' place. "Is that where Vanessa Voss lives?"

The lady's smile faded a bit. "Yes. You just missed her husband, actually."

"What's his name?" Claire asked. "I'm drawing a

blank..."

"Dominic."

Claire and Fran exchanged an uneasy look.

"You say we just missed him?" Fran said.

"Yes, only minutes ago."

Claire swallowed a bit of nausea climbing up. "So, Vanessa's home then?"

The lady gave Claire and Fran an odd look that gradually became suspicious. "How do you two know Vanessa?"

Fran smiled. "From school. It's been years though. We're here in Nashville on business and thought we'd surprise her."

The lady's suspiciousness faded. "Oh, that's sweet. I guess you haven't heard then."

"Heard?"

"Vanessa had a breakdown about two years ago now. Tried to kill Dominic and commit suicide. It was a mess. She's locked up in a mental institute. Despite it all, Dominic has stuck by her. Even though he took a job in Chattanooga, he still comes about every two weeks to check out their house and to visit her. What an amazing man." The lady offered another sweet smile. "Shall I tell him you two were here?"

Stiffly, Claire backed away. "No, that's okay. Thank you for your time."

Back in the car, Claire and Fran sat, not speaking. More nausea swelled in Claire's throat. She opened the car door and threw up. Fran handed her water, and Claire swished her mouth and spit.

Fran started the car.

Claire closed the door and took a second to breathe. When she felt a bit steadier, she said, "Do you have the contact info for the private investigator our firm uses?"

"Yes."

"Good, I'm hiring him."

On Sunday, Claire still felt sick. But she spent the day with Brian and Kelsey, concentrating on not thinking about Dominic and focusing all of her energy on her family because tomorrow she moved into the hotel and did not know when she might see them next.

They opted for dinner out at an Italian restaurant. Claire ordered an antipasto salad that looked amazing. Unfortunately, one bite in and it sat in her stomach like lead. She pushed the plate away and munched on a piece of bread.

"You had toast for dinner Friday night. Yesterday when you got home from being out with Fran you ate saltine crackers. This morning more toast. Nothing for lunch and now here you are again with the bread." Brian chuckled. "The last time you ate that much bread you were pregnant with Kelsey."

Claire almost spat the sip of ginger ale she had just drank. She felt the color leave her face and icy prickles began to crawl her skin. She stared at Brian, no words making it from her brain to her lips.

He chuckled again. "I'm just kidding. Jeez, you should see your face."

Claire's throat rolled on an uncomfortable swallow. She looked at Kelsey who thankfully was so busy twirling fettucine she hadn't noticed Claire's reaction.

"I, um, haven't been feeling well," Claire said. "Something is going around the office."

Another lie.

Brian cut into his chicken marsala.

Kelsey ate a forkful of noodles. "I saw Mr. Voss at the Town Center."

Claire's numb mind snapped into focus. "When?"

"Couple days ago." Kelsey swallowed her bite. "I was getting Starbucks with June. He walked right in."

Claire concentrated on keeping her tone light. "Did he see you?"

"Yeah, he said hi. Asked me how school was going. And basketball. Asked about you and also Dad. Even asked about Louie." Kelsey worked on assembling another mound of twirled noodles. "Everything was cool. He was really nice."

"Is that..." Claire picked at her bread. "Is that the only time you've seen him? I mean, aside from around the neighborhood."

"Yeah."

"Okay, good." Claire took a relieved breath as she looked across the table at Brian who had stopped eating and was now thoughtfully studying Claire.

She wanted to ask Brian if he, too, had seen Dominic around town but opted to wait. Instead, she changed the subject. "Looks like I'm going to be out of town on business. Maybe a week. Maybe more."

"What?" Kelsey whined. "That sucks. Where?"

"Chicago." Claire didn't know why she said Chicago, but it just came to her. She forced a smile. "The time will go by quickly, you'll see."

"You're going to miss my game this Friday. It's my first time back after this stupid finger."

"I know. I'm sorry." Claire reached over and grasped Kelsey's forearm. "You know I would never miss a game unless it was necessary. Right?"

Kelsey picked at her noodles. "I know."

An awkward silence filled the space. Claire hated this.

"When are you leaving?" Brian quietly asked.

"Tomorrow. You'll be okay with Kelsey?"

"Of course," Brian agreed, his tone still quiet and now guarded. "What about the exterminator issue?"

Crap, Claire had forgotten that whole lie. "Fran will take care of it. Don't worry."

"And the home security system?" Brian asked.

"When I get back from my trip I'll show you how to work it." Whatever it took to keep them away from the neighborhood. "You two don't need anything from the house, right?"

"I'm good," Kelsey said, eating more noodles.

Brian didn't respond.

Claire forced another smile, ignoring his watchfulness, and looking back at Kelsey. "How's the finger?"

She jabbed it in the air, sporting a cartoon Band-Aid covering the one stitch left to dissolve. "Happy to report the digit is one thread away from perfection."

Claire switched the topic again to basketball, again to school, again to June, refusing to look any more at Brian. But mostly she kept talking so she wouldn't think about what might be growing inside of her.

———

On Monday, she saw Kelsey off to school with a giant hug. "I'll see you in a week or so."

After she left, Claire busied herself packing for her "business trip."

As she zipped up her suitcase, Brian walked in. He didn't bother with small talk. "What is going on Claire?"

Like last night, she kept her tone light. "What do you mean what's going on?"

"Cut the shit."

This man knew her better than anybody. "Okay, you're right. Something is going on. I'm not ready to tell you everything right now. But I will soon. Okay?"

"Is this about Dominic?"

Claire didn't respond.

"I saw him, ya know?"

Claire's shoulders tensed. "When? Where?"

"Last week. I was out to dinner with some people from work. Dominic arrived some ten minutes later. He was by himself and sat at the bar to eat his own dinner. He saw me, even came over and said hi. He asked about you and Kelsey. It was all very civil and friendly."

"And...and that was it?"

"That was it." Brian folded his arms. "Do I need to be worried?"

The last thing Claire needed was for Brian to confront Dominic, which she knew he would do. As much as Claire loved Brian, trusted and respected him, he was no match for Dominic Voss. Brian had always been a peacemaker, not a fighter, and he certainly didn't have Dominic's calculating thoughts.

She picked her suitcase up from the bed and placed it on the floor. She kissed Brian and hugged him. Then she looked him straight in the eyes and lied through her teeth. "No, you do not need to worry."

"If I don't need to worry, then why are you carrying your gun?"

"H-how... I... How do you know I have my gun?"

Brian stared at her, flatly.

Claire pushed past him. "I need to go."

Brian watched her leave.

———

At work, Claire did not see Dominic. She knew he was there—Fran told her so—but their paths did not cross the entire day.

Claire and Fran worked nonstop to rearrange Claire's calendar. By early afternoon, she sat down with both managing partners and the director of HR. "I need to take a week, maybe two. I have a family emergency. I would also appreciate your discretion. If anyone asks, please direct them to Fran who is fielding all calls and queries."

No one batted an eye at her request.

However, as Claire was leaving, one of the managing partners said, "Wanted you to know that someone else has thrown in their hat for the senior position. We're still on track for voting at the quarter's end."

"Am I allowed to ask who?"

"Dominic Voss."

Mother fuc— Claire put on a professional smile. "Thank you for telling me."

But as she walked back to her office, she fumed.

———

By late afternoon, Claire had checked into a hotel. She'd already bought a home pregnancy test and peed on the stick. For three minutes she didn't move. Hell, she barely breathed as she stared at the stick praying, praying, *praying* for a negative.

But as the timer slowly ticked down, a positive arrived

and with it a surge of vomit that threw her toward the toilet.

She cried.

Claire Quade was carrying Dominic Voss' child.

———

That evening, Gabriel Amato, an ex-Army Ranger turned private investigator, arrived to her hotel room. Claire sat across from him, taking him in. Though she had never personally worked with him, he'd done numerous jobs for her firm and she had seen him in the halls. A large muscular man of Italian descent, he wore black jeans, gray cowboy boots, a formfitting white tee, a silver pinky ring, and had his black hair buzz cut.

He looked mean, perfect, capable, and exactly like a person should who was about to take on Dominic Voss.

Claire spent time carefully outlining the past twenty-some days, detailing the emotional and physical abuse, embarrassingly showing the blackmail images and videos, relaying all that she had learned while in Nashville, and divulging the most recent information—the pregnancy. Gabriel listened with a fierce intensity, taking notes as he did.

Claire finished with, "I would like to get protection for Brian, Kelsey, and my mom. But I don't want them to know it. Is that possible?"

"It is. I have access to highly qualified and discreet bodyguards. They won't interfere unless a life is in peril. More importantly, they'll gather intelligence. You'll need one posted here as well. None of this is going to be cheap."

"I don't care," Claire said, already breathing easier. "I

don't know how all of this works. Is there any way to find all the copies of the pictures Dominic took and the videos?"

"I know a hacker, again not cheap. She can take care of Mr. Voss' home and office computers. The copies will be challenging. He could have several stowed away—personal safe, in his vehicle, bank lockbox, etcetera... I'll find what I can." Gabriel shifted forward, quietly studying Claire. "Do you own a gun?"

"I do. I have it here."

"Good. Keep it near. I'm also going to park your car at the airport. You won't need it. You need to stay right here in this room. Additionally, we need to check you out and back in under an assumed name."

"Fine, whatever you think."

"You mentioned deleting text messages on both your old phone and your daughter's. They're still on the cloud. We can retrieve those. They'll make a good addition to the timeline I'll build toward proof of Dominic's harassment."

"We don't back up to the cloud."

"What about the SIM cards? Did you keep them when you updated your numbers?"

"No, I threw them away. I also threw away the card he gave me with the rose. I thought that was the smart thing to do. I just wanted him out of my life." Claire sighed. "I didn't realize it would morph into the beast it has become."

"I know you don't want to hear this but your home security system, that nanny cam you bought, and the dash cam on your car were a waste of your money. The man you're describing sounds seasoned. He can bypass home security, track you and your family, hack your phone or computer, scramble recording devices, and wipe out anything he doesn't want found. Which is why you have no hard evidence. He knows what he's doing."

"Then how can he be stopped?"

"Because I also know what I'm doing. However, I want you to really listen to me when I say: do not underestimate him. Just when you think you're one up, he'll be two steps ahead. I promise you that."

12

On Tuesday, Fran called. "I'm in your office with the door closed. Dominic just came by. He wanted to know where you were. I told him you were out of town on business. He wanted to know when you'd be back. I told him I wasn't sure."

"Are you okay? He didn't threaten you or anything, did he?"

"No, but I have a feeling that explanation is going to hold him off only so long."

"I'm sorry," Claire said, hating Fran had to deal with him.

"Don't worry about me. Focus on getting this guy. Any word from the PI?"

"Not yet. And by the way, I told Brian and Kelsey I was going on a business trip to Chicago. I don't think they'll call you, but still."

"Got it. I'll call tomorrow." Fran clicked off.

Claire checked in with Brian and Kelsey early evening.

"How's Chicago?" Brian asked.

"Oh, fine," Claire said, keeping her tone light. "Weather is beautiful."

"Did you see the Bean?" Kelsey wanted to know.

"No, but I look forward to that."

They talked a bit longer, finally hanging up. Soon after Claire heard from Gabriel that the discreet bodyguards were in place. Claire breathed easier.

That night—for the first time in days—she actually slept.

On Wednesday, Fran called again. "Same as yesterday. Dominic stopped by my desk, asking again when you were returning. I gave him the same spill. Where yesterday he was all smiles and friendliness, today there was an underlying tenseness to his false congeniality."

Good, thought Claire.

"I also put my own nanny cam up in my area of the office. I set it up correctly, I know I did, but it failed to record our conversation. I guess I did something wrong with the setup."

"You didn't." Claire went on to tell Fran everything Gabriel had said about just this issue.

"You know what? I don't care. I'm still going to try and catch him because I know he's not done stopping by my desk."

"Please be careful."

"I will."

They hung up. Come early evening, Claire once again checked in with Brian and Kelsey. She also called her mom. All seemed normal and well.

Gabriel called. "Some background on Dominic. His school records show excellence, testing in the genius range, and earning a full ride scholarship to Vanderbilt. No disciplinary actions were noted. No complaints. Nothing on the record. He studied computer science before switching to law."

"Explains his adeptness at technology."

"Yes, it does."

"What about his parents? Are they still alive?"

"He was raised by a single mother, no father in the picture."

"Are you going to talk to the mother?"

Gabriel hesitated.

"Just tell me."

"The mother is dead. She was electrocuted while taking a bath."

That night, Claire—once again—did not sleep.

On Thursday, Fran called. "No smiles and fake pleasantry today. He said he knew you were in Chicago. That he 'bumped' into Kelsey and she told him. I also tried to record the interaction with my phone and it came back scrambled."

At this point nothing surprised Claire. "Don't try anything else, okay? Let my PI handle things."

"Okay, but please don't worry about me. I got this."

Claire did her usual early evening check in with Brian and Kelsey. Claire didn't even have to ask, Kelsey volunteered, "I was at CVS with June and saw Mr. Voss. He asked if you were having fun on your trip and I told him you were excited to the see the Chicago Bean. I hope that was okay..."

Sneaky son of a bitch. "Yes, fine," Claire said. "All good."

They talked a few more minutes, then Gabriel called.

"We successfully hacked into Dominic's office computer," Gabriel said. "We found nothing related to you. Unfortunately, his personal laptop is not online so we weren't able to hack it remotely. We would physically need it in hand to gain access."

"Can you break into his home?" Claire asked.

"We can, yes."

"Do it. I'll pay whatever."

That night, Claire managed a few hours of sleep.

On Friday, Fran called. "Dominic didn't come into work today. I did some discreet asking around. He called in 'sick.'"

"Interesting."

"Don't leave your hotel."

"I won't. Me and room service are becoming entirely too acquainted."

Fran chuckled. "Talk tomorrow," she said before hanging up.

Early evening, Claire did her usual check-in with her family. She also exchanged a few friendly text messages with her mom. After, Gabriel called.

"He was busy today," Gabriel said. "He sat outside Brian's house and watched him and Kelsey through the windows. June picked Kelsey up for school and he followed them both to campus. He backtracked, going to Brian's work, sitting in the parking lot, following him when he went out to run errands on his free period. Dominic even went out to your mother's community and watched her play pickelball. Our bodyguards got it all on camera."

Claire's heart sank. "Oh my God. But this means we have him, right? We can prove he's stalking my family."

"It's not enough Claire, trust me. We need more to truly put him away. But it's a start."

"Does someone have to die?" Claire snapped. "Is that what it's going to take?"

Gabriel did not respond.

"What else?" she ground out.

"We used the time he was following your family to

break into his home. He has removed all the cameras and even redecorated his bedroom. In other words, if he releases those images and videos, his place cannot be linked."

Claire's mouth felt dry. "Did you find his personal laptop?"

"Yes, and it was almost too easy. It was not password protected. We copied everything on his hard drive. There wasn't much: solitaire, old papers from his college years, a spreadsheet with a home budget, and real estate specific to your neighborhood only. It's like—"

"He knew you were coming for it."

"I told you, two steps ahead. We also found several copies of a business magazine you were featured in. Between those and the specific real estate listings, we think this whole thing was premeditated. He saw you in the magazine and the fixation began."

Claire barely breathed. "That article came out 12 months ago. You're saying he's been stalking me for a year and I didn't even know it?"

"Yes, that is what I believe."

"Oh my God," she shakily breathed.

"Listen, I missed it the first time around when I was digging into Dominic's past. But Vanessa Voss is Dominic's second wife, not first. His first wife died in an accident where she fell down a flight of stairs."

That night, Claire—once again—did not sleep.

The weekend arrived. According to Gabriel, Dominic went to Nashville for the weekend. After clearing it with Gabriel, Claire spent those valuable two days reunited with Brian and Kelsey.

"Mom!" Kelsey screamed, throwing her arms around Claire.

Claire squeezed her back, feeling the relief and love to her very core. "I missed you."

"How long are you here?" Kelsey asked, not letting go of her mom.

"For the weekend."

They made the most of every second as a family, cooking together, watching movies, playing with Louie the hamster, and even venturing out. They checked on their home and even though Gabriel said it didn't matter, Claire still went through the motions of showing Brian and Kelsey how to use the new security system.

More than once Claire tried to figure out who their bodyguards were, but they remained—as Gabriel said—discreet and ready should Dominic make a move.

Come Sunday, Claire gave a final hug to Kelsey and as she exchanged a hug with Brian he whispered, "You okay?"

Claire nodded.

Back at the hotel, Gabriel called. "He's on his way home from Nashville. We have a contact at the mental hospital where Vanessa Voss is. She hasn't spoken in two years. She can barely care for herself and spends most days sitting and staring out a window. Gabriel spent most of the weekend 'visiting' with her. My contact says every time he comes, Vanessa regresses."

"He really did a number on her," Claire mumbled.

He'd really done a number on Claire.

"Also, we've located the brother of wife number one. He's in prison for murder. We requested to speak with him, but he's declined."

"Who did he murder?"

"His parents."

"Was that before or after his sister 'fell down the stairs'?"

"After."

"There are a lot of people dead in Dominic Voss' world."

To that, Gabriel had no response. Claire got the unnerving thought that her big bad private investigator was growing scared of Dominic.

On Monday, Fran called. "He just came by, simply saying: 'Tell Claire I have something that belongs to her. If she'd like it back, she should call me.' He's talking about the thumb drive, right?"

"Yes."

"What if he releases the photos?"

"He won't. It's the one thing he has over me. If he plays that card he has nothing else."

"Don't call him."

"I won't."

The day came and went. Early evening she checked in with Brian and Kelsey, touching base with her mom too. Gabriel called. His voice sounded tense. "He lost us today."

Claire's voice came just as tense. "What does that mean?"

"He shook the tail I placed on him. Claire, he's onto us."

On Tuesday morning, Fran did not place her usual call. Come lunchtime, she still had not dialed Claire. Mid afternoon arrived, and silence. Claire decided to call her instead. Fran's work phone rolled to voice mail. Claire dialed Fran's cell, and it too rolled to voice mail.

Claire got in touch with HR. "Hi, it's Claire. I was trying to find Fran. She's typically checked in with me by now. Do you mind walking by her desk and leaving her a note to call me?"

"Fran didn't come in today."

"Did she call in sick?"

"No. Just didn't show."

Claire's stomach cinched tight. "Okay, thanks. Let me call her husband." Claire clicked off. Her fingers trembled as she found Sean's name in her Contacts and pressed his number.

He answered on the first ring, his voice cracking, "Claire?"

Hot tears rushed to her eyes. He hadn't said anything other than her name and yet she knew what his next words would be.

"She's gone, Claire." His voice completely broke. "Fran's dead."

———

Claire couldn't stop her next actions even if she tried.

Knowing her bodyguard was stationed in the hotel lobby, Claire took the back steps down three flights and exited the rear of the hotel. She ordered a Lyft, and ten minutes later she sat in the back of a white four door, shaking with fury.

Being near five in the afternoon, Dominic would still be at work.

The Lyft delivered her to her office parking lot where she got out and waited next to Dominic's black BMW. Angry tears filled her eyes, trailing her cheeks. Roughly, she shoved them away. Her entire body trembled with rage.

A few office workers began to trickle out. Some saw her, pausing, giving a tiny wave hello.

Her lethal gaze stayed pinned on the front door, waiting...waiting...waiting...

Finally, Dominic pushed through, immediately seeing her and offering a jovial grin. He walked slowly toward her, glancing away every few seconds, yelling "bye" to others crossing the lot and climbing into vehicles.

Claire's fingers curled into two tight fists that shook with vehemence.

Dominic came to a stop right in front of her. "Well, hey. It's good to see you. I thought you were 'out of town.' Must be important for you to make an appearance."

"YOU SON OF A BITCH!" she screamed and punched him square in the nose.

Dominic stumbled back, holding his hands up defensively, a look of shock crossing his face. Claire ran at him, tackling him to the asphalt. Rage boiled inside of her, taking uncontrollable possession as she punched and clawed, shrieked and shouted, and cried angry tears.

All the while, Dominic did nothing to defend himself. He allowed her wrath.

Somewhere in the depths of her ire, Claire knew he was purposefully being submissive. She knew they had an audience and this looked bad—on her—but she couldn't stop herself. Dominic had killed Fran, and it was all Claire's fault.

Eventually, hands landed on her, dragging her away from a bloody and bruised, cowered Dominic. Breathing heavily, Claire jerked free. She glared at him. "You will pay for this, you total psycho."

Dominic's eyes widened in confusion. He looked around at the audience they had attracted before once again meeting Claire's gaze. "Pay for what?" he asked.

Claire broke. Hot tears rushed free. Her voice cracked. "Why?"

Again with the stupid-ass confused expression, he looked around at the onlookers before going back to Claire. "Why what?"

"Fran's dead." The words came out of her, crumbling every muscle and bone within her. She fell to her knees, the devastation overwhelming her. "You didn't have to kill her," she pleaded, sobbing. "You didn't have to kill her. You didn't have to kill her."

Fran had gone out for a morning power walk around her neighborhood and never returned. Her body was found floating in the lake that she had been walking around. It was believed that she slipped and fell, hit her head, and rolled into the lake.

Dominic's alibi checked out: he arrived at work early where numerous people saw him. Hell, even the tail Gabriel put on Dominic verified he went to work.

Claire didn't know how Dominic did it, but she knew he did.

The day after Claire's attack on him in the parking lot—which several people had filmed—he filed a restraining order against her. The day after that, he accessed Claire's email and sent the photos and videos to himself with an attached fake message:

> Dominic, I can't stop thinking of you and that one time you had me over for chili. We made such sweet love that night. Did you know I watch you through my window? I masturbate thinking of you. I follow you when you're on dates, pretending I'm the woman sitting across from you. I hired a private investigator to look into your past because I need to know everything about you. I went to Nashville to meet your wife, Vanessa. I heard she's in a 'nut house.' Sucks for her. I'm attaching photos and

videos for your viewing pleasure. These are just a sample of what I can do to you and with you. I hold my breath, waiting for your response. By the way, why did you return the red panties I gave you? They smell like me... I'll leave you with this: every night I go to bed thinking of you inside of me. Love, Claire.

Dominic forwarded that email—"with great concern"—to Human Resources who then met privately with the managing partners. The day after that, they fired Claire.

Dominic also forwarded the message plus images and videos to Brian with: "Brian, I'm sorry to send you this but I am truly worried about your ex-wife's mental well-being. Did you go through similar things with her? Regards, Dominic."

Composing a fake message and forwarding it to HR and to Brian was one thing, but Dominic crossed every line there was when he then forwarded it to Kelsey with a very quick follow up message: "Oh my gosh, Kelsey, I am so sorry. I did not mean for you to see this email and the graphic images. I thought I was forwarding it to the detective assisting me with certain things going on with your mother. Please delete everything without looking. Again, my apologies... Dominic."

Claire thought she'd moved from defense to offense, that she'd outsmarted him and was slowly gathering evidence against him. Gabriel was right—two steps ahead. Except, no more steps were required. Dominic Voss had won.

He'd defeated Claire and sufficiently beaten her back into submission.

13

Twelve hours. That's how long it had been since Claire found out that both Brian and Kelsey were contacted by Dominic. She had immediately called them both, only to have her communication ignored. Claire then went to Kelsey's school but her daughter refused to talk to her or even look at her. Desperate, Claire went to Brian's school.

He too barely made eye contact with her when he said, "Not here. Not now."

"When?" she urgently asked.

"Later." Then he went back into his classroom, leaving her standing all alone in the hall.

Now here Claire stood outside Brian's townhouse, staring at the wood panels of his door. She'd freely come and gone from his townhouse so many times since he bought it. She felt like a stranger, like she had no right to be there. She thought about leaving, but she made herself stay. A shaky breath left her as she rang the bell.

Footsteps sounded from inside, and a few seconds later

there Brian stood. She searched his face seeing so many things: exhaustion, bewilderment, embarrassment.

She looked at it from his angle. What if Claire had received that email—as fake as it was—with such graphic images and videos of him and another woman? What if Kelsey had? It would be jarring to say the least.

Claire waited, letting him lead the conversation.

He stepped outside, closing the door behind him. Awkward tension filled the space, pressing in on Claire. In the twenty plus years they'd known each other she could not recall such strain.

He adjusted his glasses and scrubbed fingers through his hair, his gaze fixed on the yard.

She couldn't take the silence. "Brian, I didn't write that email to Dominic. I can explain everything. This has all spiraled out of control. There is so much that has been going on. Most recently," Claire's voice broke. "Fran is dead. I wasn't sure if you had heard yet."

Brian's gaze snapped to hers. Claire's eyes filled with tears. Despite that awkward tension, Brian hugged her, and God, did it feel good and comforting and warm.

Sometime later, he stepped out of the hug and Claire sniffed and wiped her eyes. She looked into his familiar face, wishing he would hug her again.

Finally he spoke, "My focus right now is our daughter. She is upset, confused, and mortified at seeing pornography featuring her mother."

Claire cringed.

"She needs space."

He did too, though Claire knew he'd never say that.

"Will you let me know when Fran's funeral is?" he asked.

Claire nodded. Then she did the only thing she could; she turned around and left.

On the way home, Gabriel Amato called. "Claire, I'm sorry about Fran."

"You know Dominic did this. How did your team drop the ball?"

Gently, Gabriel said, "You never asked for security on Fran."

"It doesn't matter!" Claire yelled. "You were supposed to have eyes on Dominic!"

"We did."

"Clearly not good enough."

"I did tell you he'd picked up on the tail."

Claire's teeth clenched.

"I know you're upset, and unfortunately, my next words are not going to make things better."

"What now?" she ground out.

"Your firm sends me a lot of wo—"

"It's not *my* firm anymore," she snapped. "I got fired."

"Your previous firm," Gabriel patiently clarified. "They send me a lot of work. I was told that would stop if I continued assisting you in the case against Dominic Voss. They want distance from the whole thing. I'm sorry. I know you don't want to hear this, but I have a wife and three girls. I rely on your previous firm's ongoing business. Please understand. I'm happy to give you the name and number of another investigator if you'd like. But if you want my opinion, I would not go that route."

Her words came tight. "So what, he wins?"

"Cut your losses and regroup."

"Really, that's your advice?"

He cleared his throat.

"What about *my* family? Dominic's not going to just

leave them alone. And if we relocate you know he'll track us down."

"You're right, he will. You can't spend the rest of your life running. That's no way to live. And paying for bodyguards isn't either. Consider having a meeting with Dominic and coming to a compromise. See what it is he requires to give you freedom."

"Are you high? The man is not going to give me 'freedom.'"

Another patient breath. "Like I said, I can refer you to another investigator."

"Like that would do any good," she mumbled.

"I'm also happy to give you the contact information of the bodyguards. They're contract workers. You can hire them separately until you make some decisions."

"Yes, send those as soon as possible." She would drain every dollar in all of her accounts to ensure her family's safety until...

Until...

Until she killed Dominic Voss. She couldn't believe she just had that thought.

But it felt like the only sure way out of this nightmare.

———

At Fran's memorial, Claire sat alone in the back pew of the church—the pariah that she was.

Up front, Fran's husband Sean sat with their extended family, solemnly listening to the minister pray. Friends, including Brian and Kelsey, and co-workers occupied pews behind the family, everyone dressed in dark shades, heads bowed in respect. Dominic sat right in the center of them all, surrounded by the people Claire thought would have been on her side. Now, everyone hated her. They thought she was a bully to Dominic, not to mention a stalker, and a nympho who had shared her most private moments.

People she'd laughed with just a few weeks ago, openly ignored her. No one even chanced a look in her direction. Not even Dominic acknowledged her existence.

Claire stared hard at the back of his head, anger coursing through her. Confronting Dominic in that parking lot had set off a chain of events Claire couldn't undo even if she tried.

In her purse, the gun was nestled under her wallet. It would be so easy to pull it out and shoot Dominic right here and right now. She should be showing respect and properly grieving Fran but instead all Claire could do was fantasize about blowing Dominic's head in half.

The memorial came to an end and Claire quietly left. Outside she saw Matt, her blind date, opening the door of a tan colored Jeep. She hadn't realized he was in the church. A parking lot separated them, but he made eye contact with her, acknowledging her with a sad nod that made tears come to her eyes.

She drove home, not even looking at Dominic's house as she pulled into her garage.

Cut your losses and regroup.

Consider having a meeting with him and coming to a compromise.

See what it is he requires to give you freedom.

Gabriel's words came back to her and she rolled her eyes. Dominic had ruined her life, but if there was one thing she knew about him—he was a narcissistic dick who would not be happy until she too was locked up somewhere—just like Vanessa—or dead—just like his first wife.

There would be no compromise, no freedom, no

regrouping. This only ended one way. Claire just needed to figure out how to execute it.

Later, she sat at the kitchen island, reviewing the file Gabriel had put together on Dominic. Her phone rang. "Mom" lit up the screen.

Claire had not told her mom anything and Claire dreaded this call, but it had to be done. She answered, "Hi, Mom."

"You're alive. It's not like you to go so long without checking in with me."

"Sorry, a lot going on."

"Speaking of... Kelsey and Brian stopped by yesterday to visit. To say they were awkward puts things lightly. They avoided any conversation with your name. As they were leaving, Brian asked if we'd spoken. He also mentioned Fran died. Why didn't you tell me?"

"There's a lot I haven't told you. I just came from her memorial service."

"I would've gone."

"I know. I'm sorry I didn't think. Like I said, a lot going on." Claire paused. "Mom, you haven't heard from Dominic, right? He didn't forward you an email or anything?"

"No. The last time I spoke to Dominic was when you two were here. Why?"

Claire took a deep breath. "Okay, I have a lot to tell you..."

She started at the beginning, telling her mom about their intimate encounters, moving from there to Dominic's possessiveness and how he'd been spying on not only Claire but the entire family. She went on to describe the manipulative games he'd been playing like the lost file at work, the punctured tire, and the hang up calls. Claire told her mom about their visit to her condo and what went down in the elevator. She detailed all that Gabriel had found out about Dominic's past, how she had been living out of a hotel, the bodyguards discreetly following the family, the skill level Dominic had with technology, and she closed with the existence of the graphic videos he'd released followed by her getting fired from work.

After, Claire felt that same weight lift from her as it did when she told Fran everything as well.

For several seconds, Claire's mom made no response. Claire understood. It was a lot.

"Is he responsible for Fran?" her mom asked.

"Just like everything else, I can't prove it. But yes, I know he is. Mom, Gabriel thinks this all started last year when Dominic saw me in that magazine article."

"Have you told Brian any of this?"

"I'm incredibly worried for Brian's safety. If I tell him everything, he will confront Dominic." Claire's chest tightened. "I would absolutely lose it if something happened to Brian. Dominic is a madman. He won't think twice about offing Brian. The only way to keep him safe is to keep him in the dark. That way Dominic won't look at him as a threat." Claire needed Dominic's focus solely on her.

Her mom sighed. "I can't believe that PI guy won't help you anymore."

"He didn't say it, but I know he's scared. He has a wife and kids. At first, I was angry, but I get it. His family comes before me, as it should. Mom, there's one more thing." Claire took a breath and blew it out. Here went nothing. "I'm pregnant with Dominic's baby."

"Oh my God, Claire. Oh my God."

"I know. I've really made a mess of things. I have royally screwed up."

Her mom's voice came firm. "Now you listen to me. You are a beautiful and smart single woman who decided to have sex with a man who you thought was also single. You did nothing wrong. *He* targeted you. *He* manipulated you. *He* is the only person at fault here. Do you hear me, young lady? He may think he's some master puppeteer but all he is is a prick."

Despite the whole miserable situation, Claire laughed. She couldn't recall the last time her mom took that authoritative tone with her.

"Now this is what you're going to do. That file Gabriel put together on Dominic? You are going to thoroughly review it because that is what you do. It's your skill set. You have the ability to scrutinize every line of a hundred-page contract and find the loopholes. You analyze Dominic and find his loophole."

Relief settled through Claire. She loved her mom so much. "Thank you for listening and being on my side."

"Kelsey will come around. Give her some space. And Brian is right to help Kelsey through this. When he's had a bit of space, too, he'll hear you out."

Space that would only come when Dominic was dead.

"Okay, you have a file to review," Mom said. "Get to work and call me if you need anything. I love you."

"I love you too, Mom. Please be careful."

"I will. Trust the bodyguard is doing his job and know I'm safe. I won't take any chances."

They hung up and Claire went back to the file. Dominic volunteered. He donated to charity. He helped the elderly. On paper, he was the man of all men. Perfect, handsome, intelligent, generous...

She made notes:

- Played HS football—quarterback—earning the position after the original quarterback died while drunk driving.
- Mom—dead—electrocuted while taking a bath.
- Wife #1—dead—fell down a flight of stairs.
- Wife #2—mental hospital—tried to commit suicide by slitting her wrists.

One. Two. Three people died who were close to him. Claire would be number four if she wasn't careful. No, number five. Fran was number four.

Claire focused on wife number one: Zoe Shaw. Claire read the obituary that Gabriel had printed. It listed surviving relatives: a brother and parents.

She remembered Gabriel saying the brother was in prison for murdering the parents. Gabriel had requested to speak with the brother, who declined.

Claire sifted through more of the file, finding a newspaper article regarding Zoe's brother, Max Shaw, and the vehicular manslaughter that put him in prison. According to the reporter, the parents' car veered off the road during icy conditions, rolling several times, killing both. They were being chased by a red Nissan belonging to their son, Max Shaw.

Five. Six people died.

Claire noted the prison where Max was currently serving an eleven-year sentence. This was the loophole. Max declined to see Gabriel, but Claire still picked up her phone and dialed the prison.

14

The next morning, she left her Lexus parked in her driveway and took a Lyft to the airport where she rented a car to drive to Nashville. Roughly, three hours later she was going through prison security and signing the visitor log.

Now she sat across from Max Shaw. With a buzzed cut head, dreary brown eyes, and on the heavier side, Claire knew Max was her age—forty—though he could have passed for fifty.

"Thank you for seeing me, Mr. Shaw," she began. "I'm curious, why *did* you agree to meet with me?"

"I don't talk to reporters or private investigators. But when you said that you were a lawyer and believed I was framed, I was curious enough to see what you had to say."

"I read through your trial transcripts. Your alibi didn't hold up. I'd like to hear about it in your own words if you don't mind. You mentioned your brother-in-law…"

"Dominic Voss is his name, and he was the one who killed my parents. Unfortunately, I was partying by myself that night. I'm a recovering alcoholic. Locking my doors, closing my blinds, and drinking myself into oblivion was what I used to do. Suppose that's the upside of this place—sobriety."

"The red Nissan that was chasing your parents belonged to you," Claire said.

"Yes, but the one thing I never did was drink and drive. In fact, I would lock my keys up so I wouldn't be tempted. My car was in my driveway when I passed out drunk and it was in my driveway when the cops started banging on my door and yelling for me to 'open up.'"

"Were your keys still locked up inside your house?"

"No, they were in my car." Max leaned forward. "Dominic came into my house, took my keys, and ran my parents off the road."

"I believe you."

Max studied Claire. "How do you know Dominic?"

"Before I get into that, would you be willing to tell me about him and your sister, Zoe?"

Max visibly tensed.

"Please," Claire pleaded, letting him see every bit of desperate hope in her face.

"Dominic and I were both computer science majors at Vanderbilt. That's how we met. Unfortunately, I was the one who introduced him to Zoe. That was before I knew who he really was." Max shifted back in his chair, glancing out the side window with its bars. "Dominic hated that I was better than him at coding, programming, data structures, etcetera... I outshined him at every turn. He did not like being second best. Eventually, he switched majors to law."

Max looked away from the window and back at Claire. "There was something off with him. I realized it too late. He and Zoe were already inseparable. I told my parents that I was worried about Zoe, but they loved Dominic, and, well, I was the alcoholic black sheep of the family. Zoe was my favorite person in the entire world. She's the only one who gave me the time of day. We were best friends. They were married for five years and Dominic was like a vampire, draining her every day until she was barely a wisp of a woman."

"And when Zoe—" Max paused, losing his voice for a second. "When Zoe 'fell down the stairs' and died, I went after him. I knew he'd pushed her. That's when I really saw him. He showed me a level of evil and darkness that outmatches anything I've seen here in prison. I followed him. I watched his every move. I have a friend, a former Marine, who helped me trail him. That friend, by the way, is now dead."

Seven people gone because of Dominic.

Max continued, "I spent endless hours hacking his devices, monitoring him. The stuff I unveiled would give him the death penalty. I was getting close. I went back to my parents and showed them all the evidence I had compiled. They finally, *finally* believed me. That night, the car accident happened, my evidence disappeared, and I was put away in here. I have one year left of my sentence and I have no doubt he will kill me when I get out. That is if I don't kill him first."

Claire had not taken a breath the entire time, but she did now. It trembled as it filled her lungs and went back out.

"Now, your turn," Max said.

"Dominic Voss is terrorizing my life." Claire spent a few moments detailing the ins and outs, finishing with, "My good friend is dead. I've been fired from my job. My daughter won't speak to me. And even the private investigator is scared off. Mr. Shaw, you are the missing piece I've been looking for. All that evidence you mentioned, where is it?"

"On his key chain. He carries it everywhere. It looks like a tiny flashlight but it's a thumb drive."

Claire gasped. "He gave one to me and my daughter."

"Those would likely be trackers. If you still have it, ditch it."

An unexpected smile curled her lips.

"What?" Max asked.

"I gave mine away. I bet that drove him nuts."

Max chuckled.

"However, my daughter still has hers. I'll get rid of it ASAP."

"That thumb drive is his trophy. It's loaded with everything dating back to high school when he offed the quarterback you mentioned. You get that, and you will find everything I discovered plus everything he's done to you. The fucker sits in his creepy-ass room at night and revisits his deeds." Max shifted forward. "How did you come here today? Are you sure he didn't track you?"

"I left my car at my house so he'd think I was nearby."

"Smart."

"We live in a cul-de-sac right next door to each other."

Max winced. "Want my advice?"

"Yes."

"Dominic Voss is a sadistic psychopath. He won't blink an eye at killing your daughter and everyone else you love. If you want to stop him, you either need to get that evidence or..."

Kill him.

On the drive home, Claire lost connectivity through the mountains. As she entered Chattanooga, texts and voicemails flooded her screen.

> Kelsey: Mom, can you call me?
>
> Brian: Claire, Kelsey is very upset. Where are you?
>
> Kelsey: I know we're sort of in a fight, but I really need you.
>
> Brian: CLAIRE?!

Claire picked up her pace, swerving through traffic, simultaneously dialing Kelsey. She answered on the first ring, her voice sounding hoarse with tears. "Mom, where have you been?"

"I was in the mountains. What's going on?"

"Louie...Louie is dead," Kelsey's voice cracked.

Thirty minutes later, Claire pulled her rental car up to Brian's house. He met her at the door. Whatever tension had been between them immediately lifted. This was about Kelsey. Brian stepped aside, motioning Claire in as Kelsey rushed down the hall, crying, falling into Claire's arms. Her heart broke as she held her daughter, absorbing her cries.

Claire rubbed her back, quietly whispering, "It's okay. I'm here."

Over the top of Kelsey's head, Claire looked at Brian mouthing, *What happened?*

His lips pressed together and he shook his head. Claire continued consoling Kelsey, walking with her into the living room where they sat.

Finally, Kelsey pulled away, sniffing, wiping the tears from her face. "Why would someone do such a thing?" she said, her voice hoarse.

Claire's words came gentle. "Tell me what happened."

Kelsey started crying again. She fell back into Claire's arms. Claire once again looked at Brian who quietly said, "You know how much Louie loves to be outside on a pretty day."

Claire nodded.

Kelsey pushed away from her. "I can't listen to this." Still crying, she left the room.

Brian took a breath. "Kelsey put Louie on my porch this morning—nothing she hasn't done a hundred times before—then she left for school. When she came home, Louie had been...oh my God..." Brian closed his eyes, his next words almost a whisper. "Louie had been skinned, gutted, and impaled on a skewer."

Claire gasped.

Brian dug the heels of his hands into his eyes. "It was horrible, Claire. Just horrible."

Later, after they put Kelsey to bed and stayed in the room until she drifted off, Claire and Brian sat back in his living room, him sipping whiskey and her herbal tea.

Many, many moments stretched between them with neither saying a word. Claire thought of Louie and Kelsey, sure, but she also thought of her visit with Max Shaw and the body count that was quickly mounting. She also thought of the one thing she had that Dominic did not know about—the baby.

I always wanted kids. That's what he told Kelsey. Claire hoped he meant that because she was counting on this life inside of her being the key to getting back into Dominic's "good graces." Then, she could—

"Why are you driving a rental car?" Brian cut into her thoughts.

Claire put her tea down. "Where's Kelsey's backpack?"

"Kitchen."

Claire found it at the kitchen table and rifled through, easily locating the tracker. She pocketed it and went back to Brian. "I've got to go."

"Stay. Let's talk."

Claire backed away. "Later. I promise."

"Claire..." Brian reached for her.

But she shook her head and left.

Claire tossed Kelsey's tracker into a garbage can, returned the rental car, and drove home.

Late the next morning, Claire stood beside her mailbox, holding a manilla envelope, her gaze fixed down the road for the USPS truck. Right on time, it rounded the corner, stopping at a few houses, and placing envelopes in boxes. Eventually, it pulled up next to her home.

Claire smiled and greeted the mailman. "Hi, Howard."

"Hey, Claire. Eager for something?"

"I am yes."

Howard sifted through her mail, handing it over. With a smile, she held up the manilla envelope. "Mind putting this in Mr. Voss' box?"

"Sure." Howard gave her an odd look. "You can't walk it down yourself?" he joked.

She chuckled. "Sprained my ankle."

"Oh, that stinks."

"It sure does. Thank you," she said, "limping" back up her driveway.

The mailman continued on. Claire lingered, watching him place the envelope in Dominic's box. A sneer curled through her lips as she went back into her place.

Claire had picked a very public place for them to meet—an outdoor food court. She bought a bottle of water and chose a table right in the center of a dozen or more families out for an evening meal.

Dominic arrived exactly one minute late.

She watched him weave through the crowd, his piercing eyes fixed on her the entire time. She wished she had a picture of his intense face. She couldn't wait to see how it looked in a few minutes.

He sat down across from her, placing the contents of the manila envelope on the table between them. The pregnancy test and the note she'd written: *We need to talk. Tonight, 6 pm.* That message followed by the location she listed was sure to get him there. Claire had not been wrong.

She placed her phone on the table and powered it down. "Power yours down too and put it where I can see it."

Still with an intense face, he took his phone from his pocket, hit "stop" on the audio recorder, and powered it down.

Son of a bitch.

He placed it next to hers, looking past the table and down to her still flat stomach. "Is it mine?"

Given she'd used birth control with Brian, she stated, "Yes, the baby is yours."

"What do you want?"

"I want you to drop the restraining order. I want you to stay away from my family—Brian, Kelsey, and my mom—and I want you to move on to someone else. Leave me alone."

"Or?"

"Or I will abort this—*your*—baby."

The intensity drained from his face. With narrowed eyes, he sat back, studying her. She wished she had a picture of *this* face. She could almost see the wheels spinning. Checkmate, she thought, then corrected herself. She'd reserve checkmate until the moment she got his keychain. Or killed him. Either one.

"I want parental rights," he said.

Not on her life. "Fine, we'll draw up the paperwork."

"I want to be included in your doctor visits."

Again, not on her life. "Fine, we'll include that in the paperwork. Do we have a deal?"

He grabbed his phone and the pregnancy test. "Deal."

"I'd also like us to be civil with each other. It's not good for the baby, all this stress."

"Agreed."

Claire stayed right where she sat, watching him leave the outdoor eating area. She continued sitting there until the families that had been there left and more filtered in.

She sat, and she breathed.

Did she kid herself that he was done with his games? No, but at least this would throw a cog into things until she could exact her final move.

When she got home, her garage door wouldn't open. She parked her car in the driveway right under Kelsey's basketball hoop. As she walked inside, she noted Dominic's lights were out.

In the kitchen, she made a cup of herbal tea. She sat in the living room, staring at the TV that wasn't on. She thought of Max's parting words: *Dominic Voss is a sadistic psychopath.*

Though Claire had not put the word psychopath in the same thought with Dominic Voss, she certainly did now. With her phone she googled "psychopath" reading:

A person who is calculated and manipulative, yet charming and able to blend into society.

There should have been a picture of Dominic right there next to the definition. It went on to talk about nature versus nurture, but she put her phone down. She didn't care why or how he had become one, she only cared about ridding this world of him.

She needed to be smart. And calm, if that was even possible. She needed that stupid little flashlight slash thumb drive, sure, but she also needed that perfect moment where she would not be at fault for his demise. Though Claire was not a psychopath she tried to think like one. It was the only way to come out of this alive and a winner.

Her gaze drifted over to her purse where she'd left it on the kitchen island. Inside, nestled her gun. She'd only ever shot the gun at a range during her certification course. But she felt confident with it. She liked the weight and power in her hand.

She played out the scenario of pointing it at him. She had no doubt she'd pull the trigger. Dominic, though, wouldn't believe she had the balls. He'd welcome the challenge of "talking her down" or maybe even pushing her to the limit of actually shooting him. It would fuel his dark and calculating soul. Boy, would he ever misread her...

It would need to happen here in this house. Claire could claim self defense, and with everything that would be found on the drive, her story wouldn't be questioned.

She sipped her tea. It did not escape her that she was plotting to kill someone.

Claire picked her phone up, noting the time: 7:30 p.m. A text had come in from Brian.

> Brian: We're doing an impromptu movie out to cheer Kelsey up. Wanna join?

Though they were probably already thirty minutes into the movie, Claire texted back.

> Claire: Sorry, just seeing this. I'm home for the night. Have fun!

She waited to see if a return message came, but none did. She sipped her tea, put her head back on the recliner, and allowed exhaustion to move through her as she drifted off...

Claire groggily came to when her phone rang. Through dry and tired eyes, she squinted at the time. One in the morning? Who in the hell...?

She didn't recognize the number but she noted they had already called once, about an hour ago. Claire sat up, an ill feeling suddenly overwhelming her. She answered, "Hello, this is Claire Quade."

"Ms. Quade, this is Doctor Gibson. I'm calling from Chattanooga Regional Hospital. Your daughter and ex-husband were in a car accident. They are alive, but they have both been seriously injured. You need to get here as soon as possible."

15

Claire drove like her car was on fire, weaving in and out of early morning traffic, gunning through red lights, veering stop signs, getting honked at over and over again.

Thirty minutes later, she pulled up to the emergency room and leaped from her car.

"Ma'am, are you injured?" a security guard asked.

"No, but my family is!"

"I know you're upset, but you can't leave your vehicle here," he said, his eyes trailing over to her car. "Are you sure you're not hurt?"

She followed his gaze, shocked to see the passenger side crumbled in.

"Ma'am?"

Claire tossed him her keys, ignored whatever he spoke next, and bolted inside. At the check-in counter, she must have looked insane because the receptionist greeted her with, "Who are you here to see?"

"Brian and Kelsey Quade." Claire handed over her ID.

The receptionist checked her ID then the roster and

calmly pointed to the camera affixed to her computer. "Just a quick picture and we'll get you back. Step on that red X beneath your feet."

Claire quickly did. The camera flashed. A printer whirred. The receptionist handed her a badge that Claire stuck onto her shirt.

"Kelsey is in Room B." The receptionist pushed a button and the door to the back opened.

Claire sprinted through. Her gaze darted along the signs affixed to the walls, following the directions. Way too many seconds later, she skidded to a stop at Room B. Her heart palpitated as she forced a breath, looking through the window, seeing Kelsey badly bruised and broken, unconscious, hooked up to machines.

"Ms. Quade?"

She turned quickly, seeing a man with light features and dressed in a white coat. "Dr. Gibson?"

"Yes." They shook hands. Calmly, he said, "Kelsey is stable. Brian is currently in surgery and will be transferred to ICU."

Relief washed through Claire that her daughter was stable followed immediately by anxiousness for Brian.

The doctor continued, "Let me tell you what's going on and then we'll get you in to see Kelsey."

Claire's body trembled. She gave a jerky nod.

"They spun out of control on I-24 and rolled two times. Your daughter has a broken leg, lacerations from all the glass, and a torn tendon in the neck. She's heavily medicated and won't wake up for some time. We are moving her to a room when one is ready."

Claire looked through the door's window, her gaze touching the leg cast, the neck brace, and all the lacerations —some bandaged and some open to the air.

"Brian has internal bleeding, a shattered hip, a cracked skull, lacerations, severe bruising, two broken ankles, and a broken back."

Claire gasped.

"He's not well. We lost him here in the ER and were able to bring him back. I don't know how long he's going to be in surgery, but our neurosurgeon is one of the best. As soon as Brian's in ICU, we'll let you know." The doctor paused. "Can I answer any questions?"

Claire's mind spun. Then it fogged. She took a moment, trying to gather her thoughts. "H-how? It's not raining out. How did they spin out of control?"

"I don't have those details. I'm sorry." The doctor grasped the knob. "Would you like to go in now?"

Claire nodded.

Quietly, she approached Kelsey's bed. Hot tears pressed Claire's eyes as she stood, staring down. Kelsey looked so small under the white blanket with all the machines. For long moments, Claire simply stayed standing, listening to the machines beep, watching Kelsey breathe. Eventually, Claire sat and took her hand.

She wasn't sure how much time passed. Hours probably. Nurses quietly came and went. No one spoke, but gentle smiles were offered. One nurse brought Claire a cup of coffee.

Eventually, the sun rose. Claire stood and stretched. A tiny knock on the door's window had her glancing over to see two cops standing outside.

With a tired sigh, she left the room.

"Ms. Quade, we'd like to talk to you."

———

Now settled in an empty room, the first cop said, "Ms. Quade, where were you last night?"

The question caught her off guard. "Um...home. Why?"

"Is there anyone that can corroborate that?" the cop asked.

Claire looked between them. "What's going on?"

"Answer the question please."

"No, I fell asleep in my recliner. I was alone." Claire straightened. "Please tell me, what's going on?"

The cop said, "We have several witnesses that saw a white Lexus chasing your ex-husband and daughter's car."

Claire froze.

"We also have CCTV footage that corroborates this with, what looks like, you driving."

"That's impossible!"

The cop took a beat. "Who other than you has access to your car?"

"No one, just me. Kelsey doesn't drive so I'm the only one." Claire's thoughts did not spin. They sharpened. She welcomed the focus. "I have a key in my purse and I keep a spare on a hook in my foyer along with all my other spare keys."

"Has anyone been in your house recently? A housekeeper, a plumber, an electrician...?"

Claire's gaze honed. "Dominic Voss has been in my house."

The cop referenced his notes. "That's the man who has a restraining order against you?"

"Yes." She wanted to tell the cop that he'd done this before—stolen a key, ran his first wife's parents off the road, then framed his brother-in-law, but she knew to stay focused on the here and now.

She saw the whole thing clear in her mind. Dominic

tampered with her garage so she'd be forced to park in her driveway. He met her at the food court, then waited until she was asleep to steal her car. Dominic probably even wore a wig to make it look like Claire. He succeeded in running them off the road, then parked her car right back in her driveway and walked on over to his house. Hell, he probably slept like a baby afterward too.

"Can I see the CCTV footage?" she asked.

The cop pulled it up on an iPad, pinching and zooming in. Though the face was hidden in the shadows, the driver did have long brown hair.

"You wouldn't hear if someone took your car?" the cop asked.

Claire sat back. "No, the living room is in the back of the house. I have a security camera mounted on the front of my house. Can I check the footage?"

The cop nodded.

From her back jeans pocket, Claire retrieved her phone. She brought up the footage of last night. It showed her pulling in and parking. About an hour later, a black object covered the camera, then around eleven the black object was removed and her car was once again visible. She showed the footage to the cop.

"We're going to need that," he said.

"Also, I have a home security system." She pulled the log up. "It shows I entered my home, keying in the code, and did not leave until I received a call from the hospital."

The cop nodded, making more notes.

"I have an undercover bodyguard for each person in my family. Mine is off the clock once I'm safely inside my home. There should have been one following my family."

"Yes, he was the one who saved their lives. If he hadn't sideswiped the Lexus, throwing it off course, it could have been so much worse. He also is the one who called nine-one-one and stayed with your family until the ambulance arrived." The cop put his notepad away. "I find it curious that there is a restraining order against you and yet you're the one who's hired personal security for your entire family."

Well good, at least someone was curious.

Did any of this prove Claire was home? Not really, but it cast doubt and right now that's all she needed until she could get to Dominic.

16

For three days, Claire lived in the hospital, crossing back and forth between Brian in the ICU and Kelsey in a regular room.

Currently, Claire sat beside Brian who still had not regained consciousness and was considered a high risk, critical patient.

His machines provided ambient noise as Claire talked, moving from one topic to another. "That first apartment we shared, remember that giant roach? You screamed so loud." Claire laughed. "And, oh my God, remember that lady who lived down the hall? If I had to smell one more of her homemade sauerkraut concoctions...it's no wonder I still don't eat kraut."

Claire shifted, caressing her thumb over the back of his hand, careful of the IV. "Kelsey is doing well. They're going to keep her one more day, probably. Her broken leg is the biggest issue, but the doctor says with rehab, she'll be playing ball again soon. You know her, she's already asking when she can start PT. They bring her by once a day to visit with you. Did you know that? Of course, you know that. You can hear everything."

A gentle hand rested on Claire's shoulder. She looked up, seeing her mom.

"Claire, baby, please go home and get a proper shower and change of clothes."

"I'm fine." Claire turned back to Brian.

"Brian would want you to," her mom said. "You know he would. Plus, you need to get your home ready for Kelsey. Don't you want to make sure her room is beautiful and the kitchen is stocked with her favorite foods?"

Her mom was right. Claire did want to get some balloons, a gift basket, wash her sheets, and various other things.

"I'll be right here," her mom squeezed her shoulder. "Promise."

Claire pressed a kiss to Brian's forehead and as she moved across the ICU, her mom took the chair Claire vacated and began talking to Brian just like Claire had been doing.

She left the ICU and took the elevator up to her daughter's floor. "How's my girl?" Claire asked, finding Kelsey propped in bed, playing a basketball game on her iPad.

"So ready to go home." She made a face, and Claire laughed.

Kelsey was questioned by the cops and corroborated that a white Lexus chased them. They did at first think it was Claire, even slowing down to see what she wanted, but soon realized someone else was driving, though neither of them got a good look.

Though Claire had been here consistently since the accident, she had yet to broach the subject of the pornographic images sent to Kelsey. Between Louie dying and this, there had been a lot going on.

Claire doubted Kelsey wanted to talk about it, but still Claire said, "We haven't had a chance to talk about the email Dominic sent you. I'm sorry you had to see me in such a compromising way. Do you have any questions?"

Kelsey shifted uncomfortably. "Who was the man you were doing all that stuff with?"

"Dominic."

"I...I don't understand."

"There's a lot about him that everyone doesn't understand. Know though that it will be coming to light soon."

"What does that mean?"

Claire kissed her head. "It means you need to focus on getting well and just like I always have, I'll explain everything in great detail once the time is right."

Claire grabbed her purse and as she walked down the hall back toward the elevator, she caught sight of the bodyguard who had been following Brian and Kelsey that night. Like Kelsey, he corroborated the white Lexus, thinking it was Claire and soon realizing it wasn't, though other than long hair he could not identify the driver.

Claire stopped in front of the bodyguard. "Any sight of Dominic in the hospital?"

"None. I've been circulating the halls." He looked at her purse. "Are you going out?"

"I am, but I don't want to be followed." She wanted to give Dominic every opportunity to approach her.

The bodyguard gave her a concerned look. "Are you sure?"

"I am. And please remember not a word of this to Kelsey. I don't want my daughter in a state of fear. You are her eyes and ears."

"I know you pulled Dominic's tail, but do you want another one on him?"

"It's not worth it. Not when he knows how to shake them." Plus, it would make Dominic nice and comfortable to know he had freedom.

Minutes later she stepped out of the hospital into a bright and sunny afternoon. For a few seconds Claire stood, her face tilted up to the sun, soaking in much needed vitamin D. Then she retrieved her cell and ordered a Lyft, as the cops had towed her car to an evidence lot.

The soonest she could, she planned to sell that damn thing.

Some thirty minutes later, the Lyft let her out and she made her way into the house. Exhaustion overcame her as she stepped into the foyer and keyed in the alarm code. She put her purse on the entry table and made her way into the kitchen where she poured herself coconut water and eagerly drank. As she did, her swallowing gradually grew slower with each tingle of realization—she was not alone.

Quietly, she turned.

Through the archway and into the living room sat Dominic, casually relaxed in a recliner, his legs crossed, silently watching her.

She should probably feel a lot of powerful things right now: fear, anxiety, anger... but she didn't. Weird enough, relief hit her that this was finally about to be over. Because that's what she knew—only one of them was leaving this house alive, and it sure as hell would be her. She'd succeeded at luring him in and here he sat.

Claire didn't bother to ask how he got in. Apparently, Dominic and Houdini were related. Who knew how long Dominic had been comfortably coming and going from her home? Likely from the start as he plotted and planned his psycho scheme.

She placed her glass on the kitchen island. Her purse sat on the foyer table, gun inside, too far away. By the time she got to it, he would overtake her. Which left knives. There in the kitchen a foot or so from her fingers was the knife block with a very sharp selection. What, though, did he have on him? Or perhaps he was cocky enough to believe they would have a conversation and then he would just leave. He could be sitting over there with nothing on him but his phone and his keys—with the much desired thumb drive.

Claire stayed right where she was, waiting for him to speak first because he would hate that. He'd want her to start this conversation. She also knew her lack of response to his unexpected presence in her home had thrown him off. Oh, he would have loved for her to freak out and scream and run.

Not today, you maniac. Not ever again.

He cleared his throat.

She continued waiting.

He smirked, ever so slightly.

She sighed, ever so slightly.

"I was sorry to hear about Brian and Kelsey," he said, his tone not sorry at all.

"Thank you," she responded, her tone over the top meaningful.

"I heard it was some sort of high speed chase?" he asked, his tone now matter-of-fact.

"That's correct," she responded in kind.

"The cops questioned me. Apparently you claim someone stole your spare key and that it could've been me?"

"It's the only explanation I can think of, seeing as how you're the only person who's been in my home."

"Now, Claire, that's not true. You had a whole security company here installing alarms and cameras. I made sure the cops knew that."

"Gosh, thanks."

Dominic shifted, uncrossing his legs.

Claire shifted, moving closer to the knife block.

His gaze drifted to the block.

She tapped her fingers on the counter.

Dominic stood.

Claire yawned.

His eyes narrowed.

She smiled. Oh, this was too good. She was getting to him and it felt amazing.

"Would you like to know why I did it?" he asked.

"Did what?" she pleasantly responded.

His jaw tightened, ever so much. "Why are you acting this way?"

"What do you mean?" she sweetly said.

He took an intimidating step toward her.

She didn't move. But my God was she beyond ready for this fight.

"Let me rephrase." He moved one more step closer. "Did you learn a lesson?"

"Oh, you mean something like I threatened to abort your baby, so you threaten my daughter and Brian and then frame me? I don't know, were you hoping I would get thrown in jail, have the baby, and you would get it?" Claire shrugged, her voice still annoyingly light. "Really no lesson learned. I mean, did you prove you're a psychopath? Yes. But I already knew that. Plus, there were way too many gaps in your plan. This will never get pinned on me. Guess you're not as smart as you think you are."

He took one more step, leaving the living room and entering the hallway. His dark energy vibrated across the space. They now stood ten feet from each other.

Claire slid the largest, most treacherous looking butcher knife from the block. The overhead light glinted off its well sharpened blade.

"And just what do you think you're going to do with that?" Dominic asked.

Claire lost all fake smiles, all nauseatingly flippant tones to her voice. She looked him dead on, feeling a blackness in her soul that she had never experienced in her entire life. "*I am going to kill you.*"

Dominic flew into the kitchen.

In that self-defense course Claire and Fran took, they learned how unsettling it was for an attackee to return the aggression rather than run. Fight or flight.

Just like she did in the elevator, Claire fought.

She grabbed her glass from the counter and slammed it into his face with the strength of all of her pent-up rage. The glass shattered, a few pieces sticking into his skin and others falling to the tile floor. The unexpected action stunned him. With the knife gripped tightly, Claire lunged. Dominic ignored the shards savagely poking from his cheeks as he threw himself at her, dodging the knife and making a grab for it. But Claire managed to nick him in the side.

Dominic spun and raced from the room. Claire ran after him. He flung things, trying to set up roadblocks—a chair, a lamp, cushions—simultaneously picking glass from his face. But Claire barreled after him in hot pursuit. Dominic ducked into the downstairs powder room, turning and slamming the door just as Claire reared back with the knife, ready to deliver a stab.

He pulled at the door, pinning her arm against the jamb. Claire yelled in pain. The knife fell. Dominic dug his fingers into her scalp and slammed her head into the door. Her vision blurred. The gap between them widened. Claire kneed him in the balls and he doubled over in pain. She threw herself at him and they crashed into the wall. Fiercely she clawed, smacked, pummeled, kicked. Decorative wall art fell. A hand towel and its holder were yanked from the wall. Toilet paper flew. A fake plant rolled across the floor. The mirror above the sink cracked.

Claire was just about to grab the lid off the toilet tank when Dominic snaked his arms around her, holding her tight, and threw her into the pedestal sink.

Claire's head bounced off the cracked mirror and she dropped to the floor. In the narrow space, Dominic came down on top of her and she thrashed and flailed. He straddled her, pinning her arms above her head, his breaths heavy as he stared down at her, his gaze growing excited as he did. Dominic closed the space between them, nuzzling her neck, shifting up to her ear, then across her cheek. His lips met hers and she bit down hard.

Dominic yanked back. Claire tasted his blood. He snarled, letting go of her wrists and rearing back, ready to punch her in the face. At the last second she rolled and his fist collided with the tile floor. Her fingers brushed the knife. She once again got it in her grip just as Dominic came to his feet. With her free hand, Claire grabbed one ankle, yanking. Dominic crashed face-first into the hallway. Claire kept her grip on his ankle, swinging the knife up and plummeting it into his calf.

Dominic howled in pain as he wrenched away, kicking

Claire in the face, sending her flying back into the bathroom and across the toilet, falling into the space between it and the wall. She wiggled free right as he pounced on her. She looked up into the mad rage in his face as he grabbed her head and slammed it into the side of the toilet.

For a second, Claire lost focus, but it came back laser sharp as she swung out wildly, the knife piercing him in the ribs.

With a guttural roar, he let go of her. She climbed to her feet and flew at him, tackling him back out into the hall. Her thumbs found his eye sockets and she pressed hard. Dominic's hands grappled up her body, finding her face, digging his own thumbs into her eyes.

She had no choice but to let go and as she did, she yanked the knife from his side. Blood gushed. She went to stab him again but he managed to grapple from beneath her and run.

Claire caught up to him in the kitchen, watching him stagger to the knife block. With a scream, she ran at him, the bloody knife raised above her head. Dominic quickly grabbed a handle, yanking free a weapon, only to discover he'd taken out a sharpening rod. He dropped it, looking up at her in horror. The expression fueled her crazed rage.

Dominic tried to block her next stab but she successfully sliced through his shirt to his chest. He pushed her into the ceramic sink, wrestling the knife from her. He held her wrist, banging it into the granite counter. The pain made her release her grip, but she shoved him hard, and he stumbled back. She leaped past him, grasped another knife, and spun. Only slightly did it register he now had her original weapon and was just about to stab her as she seated the second knife into his gut.

Time suspended. Wordlessly, he stared at her as his

knife tumbled from his fingers. Claire kept a firm grip on hers. Slowly, deliberately, almost ritualistically, she tugged upward while pushing it further in. The hot slickness of his blood coated her fingers.

He maintained focus on her as he slumped to his knees, gradually falling onto the floor. She followed his movement, her grip firm. An eerie quiet settled over the kitchen. She watched his eyes, clinging desperately to life, eventually having no choice but to give in and let hell take him.

17

With one hand on her nine-month belly, Claire stood in the driveway, watching the moving van pull away from her recently sold home.

Kelsey came from the garage, a box grasped loosely in her hands. "Oh, shoot. I didn't realize they were leaving."

Claire nodded down to the street where her new blue SUV was parked. "Just put it in there."

As Kelsey passed her to do just that, Claire turned to see Brian, back brace on and cane in hand, standing on the front porch. Claire went to join him.

It had been a roller coaster of nine months. Claire did retrieve the key chain with the flash drive off of Dominic's dead body, which she turned over to the police. Max Shaw had been right. That drive contained everything, dating back to Dominic as a teenager, chronicling every thought, action, plan, and evidence to prove everything that he had done and everyone who he had manipulated, deceived, and murdered.

Max Shaw was released from prison, his record expunged. While Vanessa Voss was still in an institution, she'd made significant strides in healing with Oscar—who had been hers originally—by her side as a service dog. And though Claire's firm did acknowledge their mishandling of the situation, they did not offer Claire her job back and, truthfully, Claire felt fine with that.

It was time to start fresh.

Kelsey earned a full ride scholarship to the University of Tennessee in Knoxville. She asked Claire and Brian to move to the area and they happily agreed. Soon she would open her doors to "Claire Quade, Esquire" and Brian took a job at a private high school.

She'd also made the decision to have Dominic Voss' baby and had picked a lovely couple to adopt the boy or girl, Claire didn't know yet. But any day now the baby would be there and the couple would finally have the family they had so longed for.

On the porch, she smiled at Brian. "You doing okay?" His recovery had not been easy and his days were filled with constant pain.

But as usual, he smiled back. "I'm doing great."

Kelsey found a basketball in the SUV and dribbled up the driveway to the basket still mounted above the garage. Together Claire and Brian watched their daughter shoot hoops.

Claire felt thankful that Brian and Kelsey were there, they were all alive, and still a family.

EPILOGUE
TWENTY YEARS LATER

Claire sat on a park bench watching her five-year-old grandson, Tate, play with his best buddy. She smiled, listening to them giggle.

A gorgeous springtime sun illuminated the park. She lifted her face, smiling at the warmth coating her cheeks. She'd recently retired and spent her days doing just this—enjoying being a grandmother.

Kelsey and her husband, both teachers, were celebrating their tenth wedding anniversary on a weekend trip to Gatlinburg. When they asked Claire to watch Tate, Claire didn't hesitate to say yes. She never minded the energy Tate required.

A text came in.

> Brian: You, Matt, and Tate want to come over for burgers? Jenny's making that pasta salad you like.

> Claire: Sounds great!

Brian got remarried to a lovely woman. He and Jenny

would celebrate fifteen years in a few months. Matt relocated to Knoxville with his work ten years earlier and though he and Claire had kept in touch over the years, they didn't actually begin dating until his move. Fast-forward and the two were in a committed relationship and had been living together going on eight years now.

A shadow shifted across Claire as a man came to stand in front of her, blocking the sun and also obscuring his face.

"Excuse me," he said. "Are you Claire Quade?"

"I am, yes." Claire shifted, trying to see the man's face but he stayed right where he was, blocking the sun. "May I help you?" she asked.

His body rotated, allowing the sun to pass him. Claire squinted, holding her hand up. Gradually though, her eyes adjusted.

The man had short dark hair, neatly styled, green eyes, and a trim beard. One corner of his mouth lifted into an all-too-familiar smile.

Softly, Claire gasped.

"My name is Parker, and you are my birth mother."

ABOUT THE AUTHOR

S. E. Green is the award-winning and best-selling author of young adult and adult fiction. She grew up in Tennessee where she dreaded all things reading and writing. She didn't even read her first book for enjoyment until she was twenty-five. After that, she was hooked! When she's not writing, she's usually traveling or hanging out with a rogue armadillo that frequents her coastal Florida backyard.

BOOKS BY S. E. GREEN

Run

Before Then Now

Ten Years Later

The Family

Sister Sister

Silence

Unseen

The Lady Next Door

The Strangler

The Suicide Killer

Monster

The Third Son

Vanquished

Mother May I

Printed in Great Britain
by Amazon